MANHATTAN

GOVERNORS
ISLAND

Third Ave.
Second Ave.
First Ave.
Ave. A

Henry St.

Madison St.

East River

Atlantic Ave.

Franklin Ave.
Bedford Ave.
Nostrand Ave.
Fulton St.
Tompkins Ave.
Hancock St.

FLATBUSH

BROOKLYN BRIDGE MAP KEY

1. Brooklyn Bridge
2. 404 Tompkins Avenue
3. The Queen's apartment
4. Aunt Mouse and Aunt Beast's apartment
5. Uncle Meyer's apartment
6. Prospect Park
7. Washington Park
8. Luna Park

BROOKLYN
BRIDGE

BROOKLYN

BRIDGE

A NOVEL BY

KAREN HESSE

FEIWEL AND FRIENDS
NEW YORK, NY

A Feiwel and Friends Book
An Imprint of Macmillan

Library of Congress Cataloging-in-Publication Data

Hesse, Karen.
Brooklyn Bridge/Karen Hesse.
p. cm.
Summary: In 1903 Brooklyn, fourteen-year-old Joseph Michtom's life
changes for the worse when his parents, Russian immigrants, invent the
teddy bear and turn their apartment into a factory, while nearby the glitter
of Coney Island contrasts with the dismal lives of children dwelling
under the Brooklyn Bridge
ISBN-13: 978-0-312-37886-8 / ISBN-10: 0-312-37886-6
[1. Coming of age—Fiction.   2. Family life—New York (State)—Brooklyn—
Fiction.   3. Teddy bears—Fiction.   4. Social classes—Fiction.   5. Homeless
persons—Fiction.   6. Immigrants—Fiction.   7. Russian Americans—Fiction.
8. Jews—United States—Fiction.   9. Brooklyn (New York, N.Y.)—History—
20th century—Fiction.]   I. Title
PZ7.H4364Bro 2008   [Fic]—dc22   2008005624

Feiwel and Friends logo designed by Filomena Tuosto

First Edition: September 2008

10 9 8 7 6 5 4 3 2 1

www.feiwelandfriends.com

The captions appearing on pages 16, 32, 56, 72, 88, 105, 111, 136,
150, 158, 164, 180, and 223 are modified excerpts from
the *New York Times* and the *Brooklyn Daily Eagle* of 1903 and 1904.

For my brother, Mark, builder of bridges

We build too many walls and not enough bridges.

—ISAAC NEWTON

JULY 1903

CHAPTER ONE

THE GUYS SAY I'M LUCKY. That I got everything.

They're right. I am lucky.

I'm the luckiest kid in the world.

Not everyone's so lucky. I know this.

Take Dilly Lepkoff. Dilly pushes his cart past our store every day, rain or shine. Dilly, in his long apron, he calls, "Pickles! Pickles!" Just hearing his voice I'm drooling, tasting the garlic and vinegar across my tongue. Those pickles of Dilly's, they suck the inside of your cheeks together. They make the spit go crazy in your mouth.

So Dilly, he knows what he's doing with a pickle. But is he lucky? That all depends on what you call luck. He and his family, they been to Coney Island, which I have not. That makes him lucky in my book. But Dilly Lepkoff, he's still looking for a land of gold.

In the Michtom house we got golden land coming out our

ears. Does that make me lucky? Ever since school let out I been asking Papa to go to Coney Island. And always the same answer. "We're too busy, Joseph. Maybe next month."

ON THE CORNER of Tompkins and Hancock, Mr. Kromer's clarinet cracks its crazy jokes. Mr. Kromer plays that clarinet all day. He stands under the grocer's awning in his gray checked vest and he plays good. Makes you smile. Makes your feet smile. I hear it, even when I'm playing stickball with the guys halfway down Hancock. Even when I'm planning how to sneak into Washington Park to watch the Superbas. I hear it. Mr. Kromer really knows how to stir up something with that clarinet.

But does that make him lucky? In Russia he played clarinet for important people. Now he plays on a street corner in Brooklyn and he keeps the clarinet case open for people to drop coins. I'm not sure, but if you asked Mr. Kromer I don't think he'd say he's so lucky.

Papa, he's lucky. He doesn't work for coins anymore. We're not greenies. Not anymore. Papa, he's been in America sixteen years.

"And I didn't have a penny when I got here."

"You had to have something, Papa. How could you live if you're dead broke."

"I lived, Joseph. I'm here, am I not?" Papa says. "And I had nothing." Only he says "nuh-tink."

You get used to it. Everybody got an accent in Brooklyn.

Everybody talks a little different. Papa says he doesn't hear a difference but I do. Same as I hear Mr. Kromer's clarinet. You gotta listen.

I can't remember living anywhere but Brooklyn. Only here, above the store, in this crowded flat. Me, Mama, Papa. My kid sister, Emily. My little brother, Benjamin. I like coming home to this place. At least I used to like it. Back when we sold things like toys and cigars and paper, back before we turned the candy shop into a bear factory. Our novelty store with the big glass window, it's always been like an open book. The whole block, like a row of glass books on a long cement shelf. Even though lately we don't fix up the display window, I guess I still like coming home to it.

Some kids, they never want to go home. This time last year I didn't get it. How could anyone not want to go home? I get it now.

Still, I'm lucky. My life, it's better than most guys have it. I got plenty to eat. I got Mama and Papa both. And they don't hit. So even though I can't turn around without bumping into someone, even though I'm always tripping over the ladies who come in to sew, even though most of my time I spend inspecting, sorting, and packing bears, even though my parents don't have time anymore for me, my sister, my brother, even though the guys in the neighborhood act different with me now, I guess I'm still lucky.

But I miss the old times. Every Thursday night I would clean out the shop window. And every Friday morning Papa'd set up the new one. While Brooklyn slept Papa turned the window of Michtom's Novelty Store into a candy fantasy. That's Michtom, rhymes with "victim," which is what Papa was in Russia, where the political bear was always at the throat of the Jews, but is not what he is now. In the Old Country all Michtoms were victims but here in Brooklyn we found the land of gold. In Brooklyn we got everything. Well, nearly everything.

Papa, all he has left of his entire family is three sisters. The Queen, Aunt Beast, and Aunt Mouse. That's not their real names. It's just what my sister, Emily, and I call them. The oldest, Aunt Golda, The Queen, she's like a mother to Papa. He would like if she would come to Brooklyn to visit once in a while, but she never does. Papa's sisters, they live on the Lower East Side, in Manhattan, and they don't cross the river. Aunt Beast hates the river. Hates it. Well, I'm not crazy about it, either. No one in our family is. But at least we cross to visit them. The aunts, they never come to see us.

In my opinion Uncle Meyer more than makes up for our lack of visiting Michtom aunts. Uncle Meyer is Mama's brother. Mama pretty much raised Uncle Meyer on her own. Now he lives a seven-minute walk from here, down on Fulton. But he's over at our place all the time.

Uncle Meyer is a free thinker. He, Mama, Papa, they sit around the kitchen table. Yakita, yakita. The world twists its ankle in a pothole, Uncle Meyer calls a meeting. I stick around when Uncle Meyer comes. I keep my mouth shut and my ears open, packing stuffed bears, or cutting mohair, whatever needs doing. I don't even think about slipping away when Uncle Meyer comes. You can learn a lot from grown-ups sitting around a kitchen table. Used to be they spent hours there, but lately we can hardly find the kitchen table. Mama and Papa and their bear business. It's everywhere.

So these days, when Uncle Meyer tells me, "Pull up a chair, Joseph," you bet I do, even if the neighborhood guys are waiting a game for me, which they never used to do and which you'd think would make me happy. Except if they're waiting a game for me and I'm late or I don't show at all, they're angry. They used to just start playing as soon as enough guys showed up on the street. If I made it, great. If I didn't, well, that was okay, too. I liked it better that way. I don't like too much attention on me.

At home I work. I listen. I look. At breakfast, Uncle Meyer drinks Mama's tea, barely letting it cool. I don't know how he does it. He bolts down that scalding tea like a man dying of thirst, then drums his fingers on the empty china. His fingers are like bananas. Not the color. The shape. Long fingers. I look at my hands and hope they finish up like Uncle Meyer's. Papa's hands are okay. But they're small, like lady hands. And they smell like vanilla. I don't want little, sweet-smelling hands like Papa. I want hands that can wrap around a baseball and send it whistling over home plate. Strike-out hands. That's what I want. That's what Uncle Meyer's got.

Uncle Meyer, I don't know why, but he never married.

He's younger than Mama but at thirty, he's looking kind of old to me. I don't know. Maybe he's such a free thinker, he thinks marriage would get in his way.

He's not single due to lack of free-thinking females. There's no shortage of them in Brooklyn. In the Michtom house alone we got two, Mama and Emily. Mama. She's the freest thinker I know. She's Papa's princess. Has her way in everything. On the occasions when she and Papa disagree, Mama sends me and Emily out of the room with Benjamin. "Let me have a moment with your father," she'll say. She never yells, she never nags. As the door closes, I hear, "Now, Morris . . ." and then her voice goes a little up, a little down, a little soft, a little warm, and then comes the laughter, "the laughter of Mama's victory," Emily calls it, and when we come back into the kitchen Mama is perched on Papa's lap, her head tucked into his neck, her skirt draped over his legs, and Papa, he is so bewitched by Mama he doesn't know even the day of the week anymore.

No one is immune to Mama. Her thick brown hair, when she lets it loose, curls down her back. Long, soft curls, the color of chocolate. All of us, we do whatever it takes to make Mama happy.

Papa was smart to marry her. That's just one way Papa's smart. In sixteen years he rose from the crowd of penniless greenhorns on the Lower East Side of Manhattan, to independent shopkeeper of Brooklyn, to successful bear manufacturer, to correspondent of presidents. Well, one president. Theodore Roosevelt.

But that's all as much to do with Mama as with Papa. Mama, she's not much for cooking. She's not much by the housekeeping, either, but Mama, most of the time she knows what people want. When the guys say I'm lucky, they can't imagine the half of it. Mama knows what people want and she knows what to do about it.

Sometimes Mama figures it out by accident. That's how it happened, our big break with the bears. Who knew? This past winter, when Mama and Papa sat around the kitchen table reading the paper and saw that cartoon, the one about President Roosevelt refusing to shoot the bear cub in Mississippi, who knew how that one picture would change our lives? Maybe if I'd known I might have hid the paper that day so they never saw it. But I didn't, I didn't know.

Five months ago we were just another family in Brooklyn. Papa sold cigars, candy, writing paper, occasionally a stuffed toy made by Mama. We weren't rich, but we managed. And then they saw the cartoon in the paper.

And that night Mama set the fabric down on the kitchen table. A couple yards of medium-length brown mohair. Papa sketched out roughly what he had in mind and Mama made the pattern: a wide head coming down to a pointed muzzle, round ears, tapered feet. Papa and I did the cutting. Mama did the sewing. Emily, the stuffing. Benjamin, the drooling. We finished two stuffed bears that night, jointed at the arms and legs. Mama stitched thread claws to make the bears look more real. The eyes she designed to resemble Benjamin's.

Big and brown. The combination of those eyes and ears, those bears, I guess you could say they looked . . . thoughtful. Who knew "thoughtful" could be so appealing in a stuffed bear?

We should have guessed we were on to something. Benjamin reached his pudgy hands out and did the gimme, gimme with his fingers as Mama sewed up the last stitches on the first bear. She snipped the thread and handed the toy over to Benjamin. That's why she had to make the second bear. Benjamin wouldn't let go of the first.

That was February, five months ago. The moon shone through the shop window. I remember how bright the moon shone as I cleaned out the old display.

And then it was Friday morning. Papa rose earlier than usual, reached into the crib, and slipped the bear out from under Benjamin's arm. Benny whimpered in his sleep but didn't wake. With a bear in each hand, Papa crept downstairs, slipped quietly outside, took the two steps to the shop, and unlocked the door.

It was Brooklyn winter, before dawn. Everything shivered, that's what Papa said. It reminded him of Russia. And thoughts of Russia stirred memories of the Russian bear, symbol of a country that hated its Jews. *That* Russian bear was so different from these innocent things Papa held now under each arm. He was thinking about how his sister Golda, the one Emily and I call The Queen, how Aunt Golda had saved his life by bringing him to America.

Papa leaned the toy bears up against the glass to watch as he prepared the window for them. They were good company, he said, as he arranged a small hill of candy. On top of that hill Papa balanced the first and then the second bear.

We didn't know.

Not even when Benjamin woke crying, sweaty in his crib from all the blankets, his flannel nightgown twisted around him. Benjamin, who never cried. We didn't know.

We ate breakfast together, Mama's usual lumpy oatmeal, before Mr. Kromer started with his clarinet. Before the guys dropped by to pick me up on their way to school and maybe get a free piece of candy. Before Dilly made his first pass with the pickle cart.

Uncle Meyer took the steps two at a time that morning. Banana feet on the end of banana legs, drumming up the stairs.

"We didn't have enough trouble with bears in Russia, Morris?" he asked as he came through the kitchen door in his buffalo coat. "You have to put bears in your shop window?"

Benjamin fussed at Uncle Meyer and Uncle Meyer took the baby from Mama and settled him on his lap. Benjamin patted Uncle Meyer's cold cheeks.

"He must be teething," Papa said.

"Maybe it's teeth," Mama said.

"What's the matter, Benny boy?" Uncle Meyer asked.

Benjamin wrapped his fists around Uncle Meyer's long

fingers and cried. Big round tears rolling down his fat cheeks.

"He's not himself this morning," Papa said.

"Why would you make bears, Morris? You escaped the claws of Russia years ago."

"They're not Russian bears, Meyer," Papa said.

"No?"

"No. Go back down," Papa said. "Have a look. They're good bears. They're nice bears. They're Theodore Roosevelt bears. Very American. One-hundred-percent-enlightened bears."

Mama, still in her robe, pushed the newspaper toward her brother with the cartoon that had inspired the stuffed toys in the shop window.

"See," Papa said. "Those bears in the window . . . they're Teddy's bears."

"Teddy's bears, Morris?" Mama said, beaming at Papa. "That's good! Joseph, print what your papa said on a nice piece of card stock. We'll put it in the window with the display."

Benjamin lunged for the newspaper spread in front of Uncle Meyer, nearly tumbling out of Uncle Meyer's lap.

Mama lifted Benny into her arms and studied his face. A trolley rattled past under the window.

"Joseph, take the cartoon before Benjamin ruins it and put that in the window, too," she said. "Arrange everything nice so people can see."

Mama wet a cloth and wiped Benjamin's face. He grabbed the rag and stuck it in his mouth.

"He wants his bear back," Mama said and Emily, looking

up from her latest library book, *The Peterkin Papers*, nodded.

"How can he want his bear back?" Papa asked. "How could he even remember he had a bear?"

"He wants the bear, Morris."

"Well, he can't have it," Papa said. "It'll ruin the window to take one out."

"He wants the bear," Mama said.

"He can play with spoons," Papa replied.

"Morris, a moment alone with you please, yes?" Mama asked.

Emily closed her book on her thumb and led the way to the living room. Uncle Meyer carried his scalding tea. I carried Benjamin. Emily, Benjamin, and I sat on the floor, our ears against the closed door.

Benny whimpered around the rag in his mouth while Mama's voice softly rose and fell on the other side of the door.

"Don't worry, Benny," Emily said. "Mama will take care of it. You'll get your bear back."

Uncle Meyer sat on the edge of the sofa, downing his tea. Emily rubbed Benny's back with her hand.

And then came the laughter. Emily nodded. "See," she said.

"Children, Meyer, come," Mama called.

But when we returned to the kitchen, Mama wasn't in Papa's lap. Papa was on his way down the steps. We followed him, a little train of Michtoms with an Uncle Meyer caboose. Mr. Kromer warmed up his clarinet and started a joyful song, a morning nod to the winter streets of Brooklyn.

The store wouldn't open for another ten minutes. It didn't matter. A thick crowd of children bundled in their woolen coats had already gathered in front of the plate glass. They pointed to the mountain of candy. They pointed to the two stuffed bears balanced at its peak.

Our entire family entered the shop. As Papa removed one of the bears from the candy mountain, outside a dozen earnest eyes under caps and hoods followed its path. A dozen disappointed lids blinked as the bear moved toward Benjamin's waiting arms.

Benny's eyes lit up like candles. He dropped the soggy rag and reached out his hands, moving his little fingers in a gimme, gimme.

THAT WAS FIVE months ago.

Now, it's Brooklyn summer.

The candy business has dropped off as the bear business has taken over. Every day inside girls fill our flat with bear making. Every day outside girls deliver boxes of finished bears. Papa pays fair and the girls come and go, happy.

Benjamin and his bear are never apart.

Dilly is paying for his kids' bears with pickles.

And Mr. Kromer, his clarinet sasses under the brassy July sun. As the trolleys clang past, a bear sits in the open clarinet case. By noon, most days, that stuffed bear sits on a small hill of coins.

UNDER THE BRIDGE

There are other children. The unwanted, the forgotten, the lost ones. They gather under the bridge each night to sit, to talk, to sleep. They know, they know, they know that to everyone beyond the bridge they are invisible. They pick one another's pockets. They suck on crumbs, hungry, always hungry. And always cold, even in summer with the smell of garbage gagging the air. The wind blows off the East River and the children wrap ragged jackets around knobby ribs and shiver. The luckier ones, the ones who can remember, they tell about a time before their home was under a bridge. Sometimes they even tell the truth. Or something very near it.

If lack of time or means prevents you from going to St. Louis this summer to see the big World's Fair, don't worry. Upward to $5,000,000 has been spent to establish a world's fair of New York's very own right on Coney Island.

—THE NEW YORK TIMES

CHAPTER TWO

MAMA, HER HAT PINNED ON, sweated in her shirtwaist, waiting in front of the shop for the real-estate agent to arrive. Papa had decided he needed more room for the bear business.

The man who'd moved Mama and Papa from the Lower East Side to Brooklyn had disappeared from our lives long ago, drowned in the East River. He'd been the husband of Papa's middle sister, Aunt Zelda. The story of Aunt Zelda and Uncle Izzy was a forbidden subject. No one mentioned it. I have memories of a tall man with a pointy beard who smelled of turpentine. I have memories of other things, too. . . .

Anyway, the recommendation for a new real-estate agent came from The Queen, who suggested a lady she knew named Lizzie Kaplan.

"Tell Lizzie Kaplan not to come," I'd told Mama and Papa on the trolley after our weekly visit to the aunts. "Send her away when she gets here. Don't go with her. We don't need any more change."

"We need to expand, Joseph. Be reasonable," Mama said.

"I don't want to be reasonable." I didn't want the bear business growing. I wanted it to go away.

"Can't we just go back to selling cigars and candy?"

Papa and I had a big fight then. Emily pulled into herself, pretending to read *The Jungle Book*. Benjamin whimpered in Mama's arms. The other people on the trolley minded their own business.

I should have known better than to bring up anything on the bridge. Papa and Mama and I, we always got tense crossing the bridge. By the time we climbed down at our trolley stop, Papa wasn't speaking to me at all.

Which was the last thing I wanted. I miss Papa. He used to have time for me. He used to have time for all of us. The old Papa knew how to have fun. Now he spent his time visiting shops in Brooklyn and Manhattan, taking orders for bears, hundreds and hundreds of bears.

"MAMA, WHY CAN'T we stop with the bears?"

"Enough, Joseph," Mama said, opening her handbag and taking out her silver pocket watch to check the time. "Those bears are the best thing ever happened to us. You keep complaining, they go away. Are you listening to me? That's the way life works. You don't appreciate something, it goes away. And then where will we be? Open your eyes, Joseph Michtom. Look how much better our lives are because of the bears. If we take good care of them, they'll take good care of us. Your papa thinks so. I do, too. What do you have to worry? We'll still live in the neighborhood. You won't miss even a single stickball game."

What Mama didn't understand—Mama, who understood everything—was that because of the bear business I didn't even belong in the neighborhood anymore. No one in our family did. Not now. Not with a letter from Theodore Roosevelt hanging on the wall beside Papa's and Mama's citizenship papers. Our bears were finding homes on block after block in Brooklyn, and the money kept pouring in. Maybe Mama didn't see it. Maybe Papa didn't see it. But I did. Our success, it made people resent us.

I used to be just Joe Michtom, the kid whose parents owned the candy shop at 404 Tompkins Avenue. Now it's like I got some special kind of power. Only I'm not doing anything good with it. I'm not winning pennants or saving anybody's life or anything. And all the guys who used to like me just because I was Joe, now they hate me. Because I'm Joe. The one who got the lucky break. I thought maybe somehow I could explain this to Mama but just then a girl approached. She was maybe eighteen years old. And she was beautiful.

"Is that Lizzie Kaplan?" I asked. If that was Lizzie Kaplan, I was suddenly feeling more kindly disposed to the idea of a real-estate agent.

But she wasn't Lizzie Kaplan. This girl, in a polka-dot suit, who approached with a slip of paper in her hand, she was a stranger, totally unexpected. And yet there was something about her. Like I'd seen her somewhere, on a marquee or something. She looked that good.

"Mrs. Michtom?" she asked.

"Yes," Mama answered.

"My name is Pauline Unger. Your brother, Meyer, sent me."

Pauline Unger looked like a girl who never bought on sale. She was no immigrant. She looked like she couldn't imagine crowding into a four-room flat, sharing a bedroom with a ten-year-old sister and a three-year-old brother.

I fell in love with Pauline Unger the first minute I saw her. And I fell hard. I never felt this way before about anything. Not even baseball. She smelled good. How could anyone smell so good? Everything around me smelled hot and stale. Brooklyn smelled like . . . Brooklyn. But Pauline smelled good.

That morning Mama's face glistened with perspiration, but Pauline's forehead remained dry. Only the damp curls at her neck hinted she was not immune to heat. I wanted to put her in the shop window and show her off. I wanted to hide her away and keep her to myself. I wanted both of these things at the same time. I didn't know this was love. I didn't know what love could do to a person. If I'd known, I would have worn a blindfold that morning.

Could Mama read my thoughts as she eyed me eyeing Pauline in those first moments?

"Might I have a word alone with you?" Pauline Unger

asked Mama. "Please, Mrs. Michtom. I won't take much of your time. Just a moment."

"You say my brother sent you?"

"Yes, Meyer Marshak."

Uncle Meyer? Uncle Meyer sent this mysterious angel to our doorstep? I made a promise to myself to polish Uncle Meyer's shoes for a month. I'd polish those shoes until the leather wore away and he had to walk with his banana toes hanging out.

"Could we speak in private, Mrs. Michtom?"

"Emily, Joseph, take Benjamin over to listen to Mr. Kromer. Keep a close watch on your little brother, you hear?"

Wait a minute. Wait just one minute. Mama couldn't send me away like I was a kid. I was fourteen, after all. I was spending my summer cutting, sorting, packing bears for her night and day. With Papa gone, peddling stuffed toys to fancy shops in Manhattan, wasn't it my duty to be the man of the house? Should I be cast aside on the street to mind a baby while important discussions concerning my family were taking place?

"Mama, I could maybe be of some help here?"

Oh, she knew what I wanted. Obviously she didn't care. She raised her right eyebrow, just that one, only for a moment. She arched it high, so high. That eyebrow, it spoke a language all its own and to me, at that moment outside Michtom's Novelty Store, Mama's eyebrow said, "Enough, Joseph."

Emily and I took turns. First she and Benjamin stood in front of Mr. Kromer while I edged close to Mama and Pauline as they talked outside the shop. Then I listened to Mr. Kromer with Benjamin while Emily eavesdropped.

Brooklyn bustled around us and Mama and Pauline kept their voices low. With adults, the lower the voice, the more interesting the conversation. I didn't catch more than three, four words. Emily heard even less. Whatever it was Pauline wanted, I knew Mama would try to help. Mama, she'd help anyone.

Anyway, it ended up that Mama invited Pauline to live with us, temporarily. In our overcrowded flat Mama decided she could make room for one more. She didn't consult Papa before she committed us. She knew she could handle any objections Papa might have.

Pauline, once she and Mama had reached an agreement, left quickly. Lizzie Kaplan, the real-estate agent, arrived just as Pauline vanished.

I hoped I wouldn't get stuck looking after Benjamin all day. Anything was better than looking after a baby. Unfortunately, Mama had her eye on me.

"You and Emily, you mind Benjamin together while I'm out with Miss Kaplan, yes? Take him by Tompkins Park for the morning. Later you can go to the library. I'll make a nice lunch for you when I get back. Thank you, darlings." Of course it sounded like, "Tank you, dahlinks."

By the time Mama returned, after lunch, Emily had already lost herself in *Heidi* and I was so worn out from chasing Benjamin and speculating about Pauline, I never even asked whether Lizzie Kaplan had shown Mama anything interesting.

"Pauline will sleep here, in the kitchen, on the couch," Mama explained to us, pulling out her hat pins, removing the upside-down-mushroom hat from her head, setting it atop a pile of sewing notions. Mama made herself a cup of tea and sat down at the table. "She travels uptown to work six days a week. It will be no trouble to have her stay here."

"We need boarders, Mama?" Emily asked.

"No, darling," Mama said, absentmindedly stroking Emily's dark hair. "No. We don't need boarders. What we need is we should help Pauline by being very kind and looking after her until she can look after herself."

I was embarrassed that Pauline should see our rooms, overrun with bits and pieces of bear parts. I hadn't seen the tufted surface of the kitchen couch in months.

"Do you know her?" I asked. I felt the need to keep Mama from guessing how eager I really was to see Pauline Unger again. "Do you know anything about her? Is it a good idea to bring a stranger into our house?"

"With whom am I speaking? This sounds like Morris Michtom the father. Is this Morris Michtom the father shrunk down to a fourteen-year-old *pisher*?"

I flashed Mama a plea for compassion.

"No," Mama answered. "No, Joseph, I don't know anything about her. Just the story she told this morning. But your uncle sent her. They met at that café in Manhattan Uncle

Meyer goes to. She's part of that group. Your uncle Meyer sent her to us because she needs help. That's good enough for me. She will stay until she is ready to leave."

I hoped she would never be ready to leave.

AFTER DINNER, which Papa missed again because of bear business, Pauline arrived with a suitcase, one suitcase. Nothing more. That one suitcase made me love her ten times over. Could it really be all she had in the world? Could she look like a star of the theater and still be one of the destitute? If that was the case I would love her for her destitution. I would save her from a life of hardship. But maybe it wasn't poverty. Maybe she was wise, so wise that she carried through life only what was necessary. Then I would love her for her wisdom and her economy. That one suitcase. To me it was intoxicating.

THAT NIGHT after we'd been sent to bed early to give Pauline her privacy, I waited, listened, counted the minutes until I could see her again. On the other side of the curtain separating my bed from Emily's, my sister talked about an idea she had for a library in our house, but I only half listened. After a while Emily returned to her book. I sat on my bed, barely breathing:

As Papa arrived home and learned of the situation.

As Mama had a moment alone with Papa in the kitchen.

As Pauline waited in the living room.

As Papa welcomed Pauline into our lives.

EMILY, BEHIND her curtain, had fallen asleep over her book. She and Benjamin tossed fitfully that night in our little airless room off the kitchen. Their restlessness had nothing to do with Pauline and everything to do with the heat. The sheets twisted around them. Their hair darkened with perspiration.

I couldn't sleep, not even fitfully. And it had nothing to do with the heat.

Late, late that night, I slipped out of our bedroom. If someone asked, I was going to the bathroom. But the truth was I was going to look at Pauline.

She slept on the couch, bathed in moonlight. I stared at her and wondered how anyone could be so beautiful. What secrets was she hiding? Why was she here, in Brooklyn, with us? This stranger with skin like milk.

She turned in her sleep.

I thought I was caught.

My heart pounded.

But when nothing more happened I knew better than to push my luck. I crept back into my room and climbed into bed.

Pauline, and all signs of her, vanished before I stumbled into the kitchen for breakfast the next morning.

"Is she still here?" I asked. I knew she was, at least her scent was.

"'She,' Joseph? Who is 'she'?" Mama barely looked up from her paperwork.

Emily lifted her eyes from *Heidi* to study me.

"The girl from yesterday," I said.

"Her name is Pauline Unger. And yes, she is still here. She'll be here for a week, two weeks at the most. But no, she isn't here now. I told you, she works uptown."

"Does she sew?"

"You think all girls sew, Joseph?"

"I think you don't know anything about her. You only met her yesterday."

"Joseph, what's with you lately? You used to be such a good boy. Now everything's an argument. Wash your face, eat something, and take that smart mouth of yours out for a walk. We need cigars for the store. Go to the supplier and get a couple dozen Cremos. Go. And when you come back you should be pleasant."

"Where's Papa?" Emily asked.

"Papa has business meetings all day."

"Where's Uncle Meyer?"

"With Papa."

"Will we ever see her?" I asked. "Pauline? If she leaves so early and gets back so late . . . ?"

"You will see her tonight, Joseph. She will eat dinner with us. You'll get to know her better then. Is this acceptable to you?"

PAULINE CAME HOME before sunset and ate roast chicken with her delicate hands, dabbing at her lips with a napkin every few minutes. Mr. Kromer serenaded us with his clarinet, playing like he knew we had a special guest at our table.

26

Pauline took Uncle Meyer's place. He kept away the entire time she stayed with us. I missed Uncle Meyer. But I never wanted to see him again if it was the only way to keep Pauline with us.

Why did he send her to us? What did she mean to him? Was he going to marry her? Oh, please. I would lose my mind if he married her. How could I bear to look at her every day if she was Uncle Meyer's wife? Why didn't Uncle Meyer come and take her away?

"Where is Uncle Meyer?" Emily asked. "He doesn't eat with us anymore. Did we do something wrong?"

"He doesn't want to crowd us while Pauline's here," Mama said.

"Is he going to marry her?" I asked.

Mama said, "Joseph, this is a matter for adults." Right eyebrow arched up. End of discussion.

SO THE FIRST chance I got, when I could get away from the shop, when I knew Uncle Meyer would be home, I walked over to his flat on Fulton Street, even if it meant missing out on a game with the guys. Uncle Meyer and I needed to talk. Man to man.

"Who is she? You send a stranger to live with us. Who is she?"

"Pauline? She's a friend."

"A friend? That's all?"

"She's a friend, Joseph. Why do you want to know?"

27

"I think I deserve an explanation why a girl no one knows shows up on our doorstep and moves in. Moves in even when there's not enough room for the people who already live there. Who is she? Where does she come from? Why is she at our house? That's all."

"That's all?"

"Should there be more?"

"There's always more, Joseph."

"So what else is there, Uncle Meyer? She shows up and you stop coming. I'm not just asking for myself, you know. I'm thinking about Emily. She really misses you. She keeps asking about you. She thinks she did something wrong. And what if Pauline's a bad influence? Did you ever think of that? You could be risking the reputation of your only niece. You gotta level with me, Uncle Meyer. Who is she and what's she doing here?"

"Pauline is a guest in your home, Joseph. And you are to treat her with respect. Your sister, I assure you, will be no more adversely harmed by Pauline's temporary presence in your home than by my absence. Don't you have some kind of ball game to get to?"

The way he looked at me, I knew there was a lot more I'd probably never know. Man to man.

The way he looked at me, I also knew that was all I'd get out of him. This was my fate. Lucky me. To love a woman about whom I knew nothing.

THE RADIANT BOY

Regularly under the bridge the Radiant Boy appears. His face white, delicate, his blond curls as fair and fine as a girl's.

The children keep clear of him.

New children, those recent arrivals under the bridge, they don't know about the Radiant Boy. Don't know that when he comes it's a sign that one of them will vanish and never return. Never. Never return.

But most of the children know that the Radiant Boy brings no warmth, no hope; only despair.

No one dares get close for fear of freezing to him like a tongue to metal.

He glides. Objects float around him. His memories. The children under the bridge see his memories trailing him. They hear clocks ticking, smell wet wool, feel the spring breeze blowing through a room with white curtains, they taste roast chicken and cranberry sauce. His memories. Not theirs.

Murdered.

The Radiant Boy does not know he is dead.

Murdered.

Most of the new children don't believe he's a ghost. But one new boy wonders. That wondering boy turns away, afraid to look any longer at the small figure in white. He does not see, does not, does not see the Radiant Boy lift his left hand and drag his white finger in a single motion, smooth as a wheel, across his ghost throat.

It is not a threat. It's as involuntary as a blink. The wondering boy does not see, but the others do.

They don't tell him that he is the one, the lucky, unlucky one who will leave soon and never return.

After that the new children are no longer new. They know. They, they know about the Radiant Boy and his night visits.

By night Coney Island is a blazing, brilliant jewel shining in the dark, and visible for many miles whether by land or sea.

—THE BROOKLYN DAILY EAGLE

CHAPTER THREE

IN THE END Emily got Pauline Unger's story. Emily has this way. She can make herself invisible. People say things around her they'd never say if I was in the room. Maybe, because she has her nose in a book all the time, they think she's not paying attention. Maybe they just think she knows how to hold her tongue. Which she pretty much does. Anyway, that night Mama and Papa had business to discuss, Pauline hadn't returned yet for the evening, and Emily had gotten saddled with Benjamin again. She hardly ever complains about it, which I guess is one of the reasons why she ends up doing it so often. I, on the other hand, always look for a way out. I'd rather cut fabric or sort bears for hours than look after Benjamin for fifteen minutes.

The problem with Benny is you can't take your eyes off him for a second. He runs after a stray cat and ends up in the street with a trolley car bearing down on him. When the fire wagons tear past, Benny goes wild. And then there are the automobiles. He loves those things. And the drivers, they never look out. How are they supposed to see a crazy three-year-old like Benny? And if the streets of Brooklyn aren't dangerous enough, you never know when some kid might show up, someone with a chip on his shoulder. Benjamin could get hurt a dozen different ways. And I'd be responsible. Me. He's better off with Emily.

So right after dinner I slipped out of the house over to Hancock Street, thinking no one would notice. But my sister and brother showed up before long, Benjamin holding on to Emily with one hand, holding on to his bear with the other.

"So, Joe," Emily said, motioning me to come close. "You want to know?"

"Want to know what?"

"You want to know about your girlfriend, Pauline?"

Where Gus Lepkoff can hear she says this.

I shrugged and walked away, calling over my shoulder, "She's not my girlfriend."

Emily shrugged back. "Suit yourself."

I practiced catching with Gus. But I kept missing and Gus finally lost patience and headed around the corner and down the block to his house for a chip of ice. I wiped away the sweat trickling down the sides of my face.

"So," I said, walking back to Emily, who had settled in front of the Rostowskys'. "What do you know about her?"

Emily checked on Benjamin, who was taking his bear for a

walk up and down the Rostowskys' steps. Up and down, up and down, calling, "Kitty, kitty. Here, kitty."

Emily turned back to me. "Pauline's engaged."

"I knew it. To Uncle Meyer?"

"No. To someone in Russia."

"In Russia? An arranged marriage?"

"No, nothing like that. Do you know how smart she is, Joe? She went all the way through college and she's only nineteen."

"Of course," I said.

I knew she had to be educated. I could tell by the way she cut her chicken.

"Her parents sent her to Russia. Her graduation gift. They wanted her to see where *they* came from."

"What kind of gift is that?"

"They didn't want her to forget."

"I bet."

"So she went and she loved it there."

"Nothing bad happened to her . . . the Russians, they didn't . . . ?"

"No. She fell in love with someone there. From the same village her parents came from. Every girl in that whole village hoped this guy would pick one of them to fall in love with. But he didn't. He chose Pauline. They pledged to marry and fixed a date. Then she came back to wait for him. He needed papers and things. Now he's coming. They're supposed to get married at the end of the week."

"The end of the week? This week? Pauline? Married? Where does Uncle Meyer fit into all this?"

"They're friends. They talk. After Pauline got back to New York she wasn't sure she was in love with her Russian. She isn't sure she ever loved him. Not really loved him. She thinks maybe she just loved the idea of him. But now the guy's leaving everything he knows, coming to America. To marry her. She said he looked like such a catch over there. He was the big prize. But here, she said, he's gonna look like nothing but a greenhorn."

"That's what Pauline said? She called her fiancé 'the big prize'?"

I wanted to believe the mysterious Pauline I'd fallen in love with would never steal the heart of a poor slob from the Old Country just to drive the guy crazy and make the village girls jealous. That couldn't be my Pauline, my noble, beautiful, one-suitcase Pauline. But my sister had a memory like a steel trap. If Emily said Pauline said her fiancé was "the big prize," that's what Pauline said.

Emily wrapped her arms around herself in spite of the heat. "Pauline doesn't know if she should marry him. Oh, Joe, I think Uncle Meyer would cut off his ears for her."

"So why is she sleeping on our couch?"

"She needed a place to think."

"What's she got to think about? How she's gonna dump the guy?" Now I was angry. I was angry for the greenhorn. And I was angrier for myself. How could I have fallen for such a girl? "She's not thinking about leaving the poor guy at the altar to marry Uncle Meyer?"

" 'Course not," Emily said. "She doesn't know how Uncle Meyer feels about her. Uncle Meyer's like a big brother to her. He's her friend, that's all. When he saw how frightened she was he told her she should come to Mama. She should talk it through with Mama. That's what she's been doing, sleeping on our couch."

The more Emily said, the more my love for Pauline faded. She wasn't anything exotic and mysterious. She was just another girl.

TWO DAYS later Pauline was gone. She'd moved back to the Lower East Side. To Manhattan. Back to the arms of her parents.

Maybe she still had some secrets. Like whether she would marry her Russian or not. But whatever secrets she had, I didn't care.

MAX AND KARL

Max and Karl came to the bridge a long time ago. Even they forget how long. But they didn't always live under the bridge. Their families had been neighbors in the Old Country. Their two mothers had brought them to America on the same boat. Their fathers had remained behind, in Russia, to finish up business.

No one expected Karl's mother to die so soon after arriving in America. What choice did Max's mother have when Karl was suddenly orphaned? Of course she took him in. There wasn't food enough. The landlord threatened eviction. But she took him in.

The boys thought, Max and Karl, that it was their job to help out, to bring in money. So they asked around the neighborhood and Louie said he knew where they could get cash and he'd tell them if Max and Karl would split the take with him.

So Max and Karl broke into a room on Lorimer Street and stole sixty-eight dollars and split it with Louis Fishbein. But when they brought their share of the money home to Max's mother, she raged at them in a language they were already trying to forget. And mostly she raged at Karl, who was older, and should have known better, and wasn't her flesh and blood. She blamed him for leading Max astray. She turned on Karl with a terrible fury, never thinking that in driving Karl away, Max would go, too.

That night the boys slept in the vestibule of Dr. Pflug. When he found them curled together, like two beaten dogs, he questioned them.

We're brothers, *Max said, though they looked nothing alike.*

But the way Karl looked after Max, Dr. Pflug believed them.

We're orphans, *said Karl.*

And Dr. Pflug fed them a good meal and said they could stay the night.

Which they did. In that vestibule. Without any hardship to the doctor. But the next day he called the police and the Society for the Prevention of Cruelty to Children. And the boys fled.

They wandered until they found their way under the bridge where no one fed them but no one chased them away, either. It was the first time they belonged somewhere, in a way they never had in Russia, in a way they never had in America.

They had found a home under the bridge. And so they stayed.

CHAPTER FOUR

EMILY AND I NEVER called Aunt Golda "The Queen" to her face, though she probably wouldn't have minded. She was our own private Statue of Liberty. Tall and straight, guiding us. She towered over Papa and Aunt Beast and Aunt Mouse and was the boss of us all.

The Queen colored her lips and her cheeks with paint. Pauline Unger had been what you'd call delicate. Not The Queen. She had such a deep voice, if you closed your eyes you couldn't be certain, man or woman. But when you opened your eyes you knew for sure. The Queen was definitely a lady.

She came first to America, of all of Papa's family. Something happened to her in the beginning here, something bad. She never talked about it. Whatever it was, whatever happened to her, it made her hard against men. She didn't like them, not any of them. Except, of course, for Papa. And me. And Benjamin.

When we visited Papa's other sisters on Henry Street each week, the visit wouldn't be complete until The Queen turned up as a topic of conversation. As soon as the aunts got on the subject of The Queen I'd be given a very important errand to run. But usually Emily managed to stay and listen for both of us.

The Queen had saved every penny she'd made when she got to this country and one by one she had brought her siblings over. Papa had done all right for himself; I could tell The Queen was proud of her baby brother. But Aunt Mouse and Aunt Beast, they didn't take to America the way The Queen had hoped. They'd turned their backs on the things America had to offer. So many opportunities spread before them and what did they do? They took in sewing and they worked in their flat, never leaving unless they had to. That was their life.

Even so, I think The Queen was a little envious of her sisters. They had passed their citizenship tests long ago. The Queen had never gotten around to taking hers.

CHILDREN GOT some sort of special exemption from The Queen's general scorn. And of the three of us, I occupied the place of honor at The Queen's table. I liked visiting her because she made me feel smart, like I couldn't ever make a mistake. I think maybe she liked me in particular because I was the oldest American-born member of the family. Being a natural-born American, that was the sort of thing The Queen admired, even though I had nothing to do with it. The truth is none of us, not me, not Emily, not Benjamin, none of us would have been born here, maybe none of us would have been born at all, if The Queen hadn't paid to bring Papa to America.

Aunt Beast owed her life to The Queen, too, but you'd never know it. Aunt Beast said Aunt Golda was selfish, and brazen, and cruel. She said Aunt Golda never married because men couldn't stand to be in the same room with her for more than thirty seconds.

"I like to be in the same room with her and I'm a man," I said.

Aunt Beast snorted. "What man? You're a fourteen-year-old *pisher*. Where is there a man here? Come back in a few years. We'll see if a man comes through the door."

"Joseph," Aunt Mouse said kindly. "Would you go out and find the iceman and buy a nickel's worth?" She opened a drawer in the sideboard, removing eight cents. "Maybe you will find something else good for you and your brother and sister while you're out?" And she patted my hand.

OF COURSE when The Queen stopped by, honey poured from the lips of Aunt Beast. This drove The Queen crazy. She was not stupid. What did Aunt Beast think?

Aunt Mouse and Aunt Beast lived together on Henry Street in one of the nicer flats on the Lower East Side. They had a front room with four windows, a good fire escape, and they were nearest the toilet on a floor with only two other flats. Though their flat was plenty large, The Queen refused to live with them. She had a small room of her own on Madison. She made raincoats at a factory in the Bronx. The Queen earned very good money and if you believed Aunt Beast, she spent all of it on makeup.

"What's she trying to do," Aunt Beast asked. "Get a man? Who gets a man like that? Especially at her age. She paints her face like a clown."

Aunt Mouse, the peacemaker, said, "Not like a clown exactly."

ONE DAY during our weekly visit to Henry Street, sitting in the parlor on the tapestry sofa with its sharp steel springs, Mama and I listened, sweating, as Aunt Beast and Aunt Mouse told Michtom family stories. Aunt Beast turned to me and held me in her gaze.

"Joseph," she said. "Would you be good enough to run over to Madison and ask my sister to give you the family samovar? I miss that thing like nobody's business. It's like we have Mama in the room if we have the samovar. We'll place it in the center of the table. Here."

"Come right back, Joseph," Mama called uneasily as I started out the door. "As soon as you finish at Aunt Golda's."

I HURRIED over to Madison, took the stairs two at a time and knocked at The Queen's oak door.

Mrs. Greene from next door poked her head out, saw it was me, and waved. Just as silently as she had appeared,

43

Mrs. Greene vanished again, afraid Aunt Golda should catch her snooping.

From inside The Queen's room came the familiar deep voice. "Who is it?"

"It's me. Joseph."

"Joseph Michtom? Son of my famous brother, Morris?"

Always. Even before the bears. Always when I came she asked the same question, always in the same way. To which I always answered, "At your service."

"Ah, Joseph," The Queen said, ushering me in.

I entered and sat at the little table that served as dressing table, dining room table, sewing table, reading table, and anything else The Queen needed it for. It was good to be with her. I felt myself relax. I smiled.

"And to what do I owe this unexpected pleasure?" Aunt Golda said, smiling back.

She offered me a dish filled with hard candy. I'd spent so many years sorting, pricing, selling candy. Most guys, they'd have filled their fists and their pockets with the stuff The Queen had in that dish. I could take it or leave it.

"No, thanks," I said, waving my hands like a referee calling safe.

"So, Joseph. If you didn't come for candy, what then?"

"I've been sent to fetch the samovar," I said.

"The samovar?"

"Aunt Zelda wants to have the family samovar on Henry Street."

"That samovar . . . our mother lost her life because of that damned thing. Would she give it up when the Cossack tried to take it? No. Rather she should have her jaw broken. I don't have the samovar, Joseph. I sold it. Years ago. *Ach*, my sisters think the samovar was a treasure. It was not a treasure. That samovar had nothing but sadness in it. A cup of tea made in that samovar had the blood of our mother in it. They should not drink from such sorrow, my sisters, even if they do drive me crazy."

"What should I tell them?"

"What do they need with a samovar? Tell Zelda she should stick her tongue in her teacup to boil her water. That tongue of hers is hot enough. Tell her that, Joseph."

I hoped my luck would hold long enough that I should survive to my fifteenth birthday.

"So, how's everyone in Brooklyn? Emily, Benjamin. Everyone good?"

We talked for a while about the family, Papa and Mama and the bears, the dwindling interest in the candy shop.

And then I told The Queen about Pauline Unger. I couldn't speak to Uncle Meyer about Pauline. I didn't even know why I was still thinking about her. Pauline. But here, in the safety of The Queen's room, I talked.

"Maybe I would have fallen in love with the real-estate agent you sent to us if she'd come first. But she didn't. I don't know, Tante Goldie. It was a morning of beautiful women. Maybe I didn't have a choice. It was my morning to lose my mind."

"This Pauline was your first love, Joseph?"

I blushed, nodding.

The Queen laughed. "It's good you got that first time over with. You have a clever head on your shoulders, my nephew. Try not to lose it again over a girl. But if you have to . . . Well, just try not to."

BACK ON HENRY Street the aunts wanted to know every detail, every word out of The Queen's mouth. I told them as little as possible.

"What did she say about the samovar?" Aunt Beast asked.

"She said you couldn't have it."

"Selfish. Didn't I say she was selfish? What else did she say?"

The couple in the next flat started yelling. Aunt Beast rapped on the wall for silence.

"She gave me some advice," I said.

"Advice. That she's got plenty of. That and makeup," Aunt Beast said.

The argument next door started up again. Aunt Beast, looking indignant, pounded harder. If she'd hit the wall with any more force, her fist would've gone through it. Luckily, the yelling next door stopped and didn't start again.

"It's not natural to live alone," Aunt Beast said. "What? Is she too good for us?"

"But you don't want Aunt Golda to live with you, do

you?" I asked. I turned to Mama, who shrugged, looking eager to leave, to get back to Brooklyn and all the work waiting for her there.

I didn't understand Aunt Beast. Maybe Mama knew what people wanted but I didn't have any idea. Particularly when it came to Aunt Beast. She frightened me. Mama and Papa made excuses for her but still . . .

"Of course we don't want Golda living with us. She would drive us screaming into the street. But it's unnatural that she wouldn't want to try. She doesn't even come here."

"She comes sometimes," Aunt Mouse said. "And she's so generous. She sends the grocer with a box of food for a surprise."

"Of course she does," Aunt Beast answered. "When she knows the children are coming."

"And she helps us with the rent," Aunt Mouse added.

"What else? You think she wants her sisters living in a hovel? Or worse yet, out on the street, homeless? You think she brought us here from Russia to languish in the poorhouse? Of course she helps with the rent. When she has anything left over from her cosmetics purchases."

IN OUR ROOM that night, Emily and I talked softly, the curtain separating us. She had stayed in Brooklyn to take care of Benjamin, whose nose had been running, while I went to Henry Street with Mama, but she wanted to know all about my day on the Lower East Side. Emily liked details. She said that's why she loved books. Because of the details. I related the twists and turns of my visit to the aunts.

Emily whispered so as not to wake Benjamin, "Aunt Beast used to wear cosmetics, too."

"How do you know?"

"I heard Mama talking with Papa. Aunt Beast was a free thinker once, like Uncle Meyer. She wrote poetry."

I snorted.

Benjamin lifted his head, looked around through the bars of his crib, then wiggled himself back into a comfortable position, wrapping his arm around his bear and sighing. Although his eyes had opened, he never really woke.

"Aunt Beast was even married. To an artist. He sold real estate but he hated it. Aunt Beast made him. He only wanted to paint. Something terrible happened to him. I don't know what."

An artist. Tall. Pointy beard. The smell of turpentine. I knew what had happened to him. He was my uncle. Izzy.

"What about Aunt Mouse?" I asked.

"What about her?"

"Did she ever marry?"

I expected Emily to say, "No."

I couldn't imagine little Aunt Mouse ever married.

But Emily said, "Yeah, she was married, too. Even before Papa married Mama. Aunt Mouse's husband died young. From tuberculosis. That's his picture in the frame by her bed.

He was so handsome. You've seen that picture dozens of times, Joe. Didn't you ever wonder about it?"

I had wondered, but I'd never asked. Emily had asked.

Me and Emily, we both heard things, regular things, like Mr. Kromer's clarinet, like the resentment in the voices of neighbors who used to be friends. But Emily heard other things, too. Sometimes she could take bits and pieces and figure out how they fit together. Emily was only ten, but she knew a lot more than I knew on the subject of just about everything, even if I'd never admit it to her face. Of course, with Emily I didn't have to admit it. She already knew.

Emily sighed behind her curtain. I could tell by the way she shuffled around in her bed that she'd picked up her book and started reading again.

"What you reading, Em?"

"*Five Little Peppers and How They Grew.*"

"You like it?"

"Ummm."

That was a yes, a typical Emily-with-her-nose-in-a-book yes.

"Have you heard anything about your library application?"

Emily had filled out an application to have a real library, right here at 404 Tompkins Avenue. "Not yet, Joe," she whispered. "Do you think I will?"

"Sure," I said. "It hasn't been that long since you sent off the papers. You just have to be patient."

"I guess. I hope I hear something soon."

"Yeah, me, too. Well, good night, Em," I whispered.

"'Night, Joe."

Emily turned a page behind the curtain.

I FELT RESTLESS. Crossing the bridge and seeing Aunt Beast always had that effect on me. What was I doing in bed anyway? I was fourteen years old, for Pete's sake, on a summer night, and in bed like a little baby. I shoulda been out having a good time. Hanging out with the guys. Out from under my parents' watchful eyes. I shoulda been on Coney Island, riding a rocket to the moon. I should have been anywhere, anywhere but here.

THE BRIDE

*The girl, thick hair pinned up in the latest style, fell into
the company under the bridge wearing her wedding dress,
all she had left in the world after quitting her job as a
waitress to marry a man she'd met through the classifieds.*

The ad said:

"Looking for a young woman with money of her
own."

The children exchange glances.

Money of your own? Did you have money of your
own?

*She nods. What a slow nod, what a slow, sad nod. A
nod that says I never knew what the world was like before
today. She sits on a tin drum in her wedding dress.*

*Without telling her mother, she answered the ad in
the classifieds:*

"Refined and gentle," *what he wanted in a girl.*

"Bright and ambitious," *what he said about himself.*

*Her mother could have read her thoughts in Danish,
but not in English, and these thoughts of courtship with a
handsome stranger were in English. She deceived that*

mother, that mother, that poor lost mother, when she answered the ad and fell in love.

He was so handsome.

It was June when they first met and almost from the start he looked at her like it hurt to love her so much. He looked at her like no one had ever looked at her before.

She could see how much he suffered when he looked at her that way. She couldn't help herself.

He was so handsome.

He took her on the trolley to Newark. They climbed down, arm in arm, and walked, and talked under an arbor of trees along the streets of Newark. And at last they stopped before a cottage.

A cottage?

She nodded.

A cottage he was buying, *she told them.*

For you?

For us.

He opened the door.

With a key?

With a key.

And he promised her a future in that empty cottage where she arranged imaginary furniture a dozen different ways. And he laughed and pretended with her. He begged her to be his bride and she said yes.

You said yes?

She gave notice at the restaurant.

They were jealous, the way they looked at me, me, Gretta Hansen, a girl with a beau and a cottage and a future.

So she couldn't go back. Could never go back. Not to work, not to her mother.

How did he leave you?

How did you know he left?

They look at her.

At 150 Broadway, Manhattan, outside City Hall . . .

She had bathed so carefully that morning, rubbing herself with rose oil. Then the clothing, her undergarments scented, satin against skin. Each layer went on. But just before she left, her mother came home unexpectedly and found her before the mirror, turning to admire herself one more time before meeting Charlie.

Charlie?

Her mother pleaded, how she pleaded.

What are you doing? Better you should take a knife and stab me in the back!

She screamed and she wept. She grabbed at The Bride, her daughter, her Gretta, who thought only of tearing loose, fleeing through the door, down the hall, down stairs and landings to marry Charlie. How her mother fought for her.

See here where she ripped the lace?

A little rip, a rip you'd never notice unless you were looking.

She ran to the trolley in her wedding dress, in the rain. So much rain, and her umbrella still at the restaurant. Her heart wouldn't stay in her chest. It pounded in her eyes, and her ears, and her throat. She would die if she didn't marry Charlie. Die. She would!

And then suddenly there he was, waiting on the steps for his bride to come, and sunlight touched her heart, even on this dreary day, and she ran to him, imagining how she looked, her wedding dress clinging to her in the rain.

He was so handsome.

Reaching his hand out to her, he caressed her face, he loved her completely, even sopping wet, dripping. She gave him all she had in the world, her trust, her innocence, and her savings, transferred from her purse to his gentle hand.

My dearest, *he said,* my dearest Gretta, wait here. I'll be only a moment.

And he disappeared inside City Hall to talk to the mayor, to make things ready. The rain kept falling. She could see her wedding dress reflected in pools of rainwater. Rain ran down the steps of City Hall. An hour passed. Rain dripped from the lintel over the door. And another hour. And even one more.

She sneezed and felt herself grow colder, and paler, until she was as white as her dress because . . .

She knew. She, she knew at last. Even she had to know. She put the truth between her lips like a lozenge and it settled on her tongue with its little barbed hooks. It caught in her throat and she couldn't swallow.

And he didn't come back.

The children knew the last line of her story before she ever began, before she said the first word, they knew how it would end.

And he didn't come back.

You can't stay in a wedding dress forever.

The children knew to protect her they had to peel the hurt away, though even in other clothes she would always be The Bride to them.

They found her some widow's black off a line. She changed into the ugly dress and folded her wedding whites, handing them to the boy with the derby hat, Max. And he and his friend, Karl, sold them for her, gave her the money.

She bought food for all of them. Her wedding feast.

Their banquet tables were ash cans.

Leaving the worries of the world outside the gate, visitors come to be entertained and to become part of the entertainment.

—THE BROOKLYN DAILY EAGLE

CHAPTER FIVE

PAPA WAS IN the middle of a meeting when he received word. Aunt Golda had collapsed on her way home from work. Apoplexy. We should come at once. She was failing fast.

Aunt Mouse opened the door to Aunt Golda's room and let us in.

Aunt Beast fussed around the bed.

In the white sheets lay The Queen. Or what had once been The Queen. The right side of her face drooped like melted wax. Even her right eye drooped. Her left eye worked okay still. She used it to glare at Aunt Beast.

Mama, at first sight of The Queen in such a state, turned and fled from the room, back into the hallway. Papa went out to comfort her.

Aunt Golda caught sight of me. She made a gurgling sound. Beckoned to me with her left hand. I approached her bed slowly.

"Joseph . . . Michtom," she slurred. She couldn't get out the rest, the part about my being the son of her famous brother, Morris.

I played along anyway, my heart pounding. "At your service."

"Everyone . . . leave," Aunt Golda ordered. "I want . . . just . . . Joseph."

"May I stay?" Emily asked.

The Queen hesitated. Then shook her head no.

"AM I . . . finished?" Aunt Golda fixed her left eye on my face, studying me. "Tell me . . . the truth."

Every word struggled through her twisted mouth.

Boys aren't supposed to cry. I made fists in my pockets, tight fists. "It's hard to say, Tante. What do I know?"

"Joseph . . . truth."

I looked down at her worn black shoes tucked half under her bed, wondering who had taken them off her feet, Aunt Beast or Aunt Mouse.

"Joseph?"

I swallowed. "It doesn't look so good for you, Tante Goldie. But I could be wrong."

"Not wrong . . . but not yet . . . Joseph. Something . . . still to do."

"What? You don't have to do anything. Save your strength."

"For what? . . . Joseph . . . pay attention . . . I'm dying."

The Queen couldn't be dying.

"I'm dying . . . and . . . I . . . never became . . . a citizen. . . . Joseph . . . I want to . . . die an American."

"You can't die, Tante. You can't."

"I can . . . and I will. . . . Listen, my nephew . . . you got backbone . . . this I know. Help me . . . help me become . . . a citizen."

"You want me to bring a judge?"

"I want you . . . you should do it."

"But . . ."

"You . . . ask the questions . . . Joseph. You."

"But I don't know the questions, Tante." Why? Why me?

"Ask me, Joseph. . . . What a citizen should know . . . you can do that . . . yes?"

"I . . . I guess. I guess I can do that."

"So, ask."

"Okay, okay."

I was stalling for time, but it didn't look like Aunt Golda had too much time. I wanted to run from the room. Get Mama, Papa. But this was the way The Queen wanted it. So this was the way we should do it.

"Okay, question number one. What are the colors of the American flag?"

"This is important?"

"Yes. You wouldn't want to pledge allegiance to the wrong flag, would you? What are the colors of the American flag?"

"Red," The Queen answered. "White . . . blue."

"Okay. That's good. First question on your citizenship test, perfect."

"Next?"

What could I ask her that she'd know? "Who was the first president of America?"

"George . . . Washington."

She struggled with each syllable. I pulled at the neckband of my shirt, loosening the top button. As hard as it was for me to breathe, it must have been a hundred times harder for my aunt. Sweat rolled down my back.

"Joseph . . . did you hear?"

"I heard, Tante Goldie. George Washington. Yes. That's right. That's two correct answers."

"How many more?"

"Three more. The test for you has five questions. How you feeling?"

"Not too good."

"Is five too many? Should I get Mama?"

"No . . . just . . . ask."

Looking down at her, I thought, She can't die. If The Queen dies, who will guide me?

"Joseph!"

"Okay. Third question. Which president freed the slaves?"

She glared at me. "It's too easy . . . Joseph. It won't count . . . if it's too easy."

"Which president freed the slaves?"

"Lincoln."

I tightened the fists in my pockets. "Lincoln is correct, Tante. Did he have a first name?"

"Yes, Joseph . . . he had a . . . good Jewish name . . . Abraham. Right?"

"Right. And now you are more than halfway there."

"Next?" She actually sounded excited.

"Okay, Tante. Next question. What happened on the Fourth of July?"

"The Fourth . . . nothing. . . . But last year . . . we had a picnic."

I laughed. How could I laugh at a time like this? But I laughed.

"What . . . not right?" Her voice trembled.

I wished I could take it back, my question, my laughter. But I couldn't. "Yes. Your answer is correct but you only get half credit."

"Why?"

"That's what happened for us, for the Michtom family on the Fourth of July, but for the citizenship test you have to know what happened for the country on the Fourth of July."

"I apologize . . . the country . . . America . . . is Independence Day . . . no more England . . . yes?"

"That is a perfect answer, Tante. For that answer you get extra credit."

"Am I finished . . . ?"

"Nearly. One more question."

Why didn't I say yes? She'd lost count. I could have said yes.

"Ask it, Joseph . . . I can't . . . stand the suspense."

I looked down at her. Drool ran across her chin. I wondered if I should use the sheet to wipe it. If that would make her angry. Or sad. Or hurt. And then I just did it anyway. I dabbed at the spit with her sheet and she didn't even notice.

"Okay, Tante. Last question. What are the three rights we all have here in America?"

Her left eye looked horrified. "You . . . made the last one . . . too hard."

I struggled to understand her.

"Too hard."

"It's not too hard, Tante Goldie." But I knew it was. I knew as soon as the words left my mouth.

"Joseph . . . it's hard . . . it's too hard."

"You know this. You do. The three rights granted to every American citizen. Inalienable rights. It's the reason you had to leave Russia, Tante Goldie. It's what your parents lost at the hands of the Cossacks."

"Life . . . Joseph?" The Queen asked.

Oh, she knew. She knew. "Yes. That's the first one."

"Liberty. . . . Is this . . . what you want, Joseph?"

"Yes," I said, my voice cracking. "This is what I want, Tante."

"Life . . . liberty . . . pursuit of happiness."

The Queen's left eye swam with tears.

"Congratulations, Tante! Congratulations. You are now a one-hundred-percent no-question-about-it, complete and total citizen of the United States of America."

I bent over and wrapped my arms around her, burying my face in her neck.

"Put this . . . in writing, Joseph . . . get the box . . . under my bed." She was taking control, giving orders. She was The Queen. I did as she commanded.

I crawled under her bed and retrieved a box.

"The key," she said. "In the drawer . . . under the mirror." She sighed.

I pulled the drawer out. How many times had The Queen applied her makeup in front of this mirror. The drawer smelled of The Queen, it was stained with face powder. At the bottom of the drawer was a key.

ABSORBED IN MY work, recording The Queen's citizenship paper, I didn't notice that she'd stopped breathing. She died that quietly. While I sat at her table, my back to her.

Some part of my brain had heard that last breath. Had recognized what I was hearing. I kept writing anyway. I needed to finish before I got the others.

AUNT BEAST AND Aunt Mouse rushed past me. Papa's eyes were so round. For a second I saw a little boy there, behind the grown-up face I saw a little boy, the little boy he was a long time ago, when his sister Golda Michtom left him to come to America.

Emily took my hand and I brought her in. Mama and Papa followed. Mrs. Lepkoff had offered to look after Benjamin back in Brooklyn for us. Benjamin would never remember The Queen. She would be more of a shadow to him than Aunt Beast's husband was to me.

"What's this box?" Emily asked. Emily was afraid to go near the bed, near The Queen's quiet body, near Aunt Mouse and Aunt Beast, leaning against each other, weeping.

"She was like a mother to me," Aunt Beast was saying. "It is like losing again our mama. Oh, what will become of us? She took such good care of us."

Aunt Mouse wept. No words. Just tears.

"Joe." Emily tugged at my hand. "What's in the box?"

"It's The Queen's papers," I said. "All of her important papers."

"Is there a bank book?" Aunt Beast asked through her tears.

Papa began sorting through the papers in the box.

"No. No bank book, Zelda," he said.

"What, then?" Aunt Beast asked, leaving the bedside and coming over to stand beside Papa. "You think her money is here in the room somewhere?"

Aunt Mouse and Mama sat down on either side of The Queen's body and each took one of her hands gently, lovingly.

"I don't think there is any money," Papa said. "This box. It's filled with receipts. Golda has been sending money back to Russia regularly. Just the way she did when she brought us out. Look at this . . . 'Sara Grissel, arrived March 1892, Yossel Basker, arrived September 1898, Ruth Himmel, arrived June 1903.' That was just last month. Look at them all. There are dozens of them. Golda has been paying to bring people out of Russia for the last twenty years. She got us out and then kept going. She never stopped. Never."

"But she didn't say . . . ," Aunt Beast whispered, looking back at the body of The Queen with awe.

"No," Papa said. "Of course she didn't."

Mama said, "We must find them. We must find them all and let them know. All of them."

Papa said, "There's more in here." He lifted out two thick packets, one addressed to Lena, one to Zelda.

"Is there one for us, too, Papa?" Emily asked.

"No, nothing for us, Emily," Papa said. "That's everything."

Papa didn't say a word about the homemade citizenship paper I'd put inside the box. I'd modeled it after his and Mama's. Could he tell it wasn't official? Did he know his son was making a meaningless scribble on paper, his back turned away, as his eldest sister died?

Maybe he would say something when we returned home. Maybe he'd punish me then. But for right now, he said nothing.

CHAPTER SIX

NEWS OF THE QUEEN'S death spread like a tenement fire. The cemetery teemed with strangers. I knew mostly the immediate family. But Lizzie Kaplan, the real-estate agent, came. And Pauline Unger, out of respect for Mama, she came, too, with her new Russian husband.

Seven days we sat shivah in The Queen's room on Madison. The Gershowitzes and the Lepkoffs took turns watching Benjamin for us back in Brooklyn.

We crowded into the cramped space of The Queen's room on the Lower East Side, with its one mirror covered in white cloth and a bowl of water at the door. Papa took comfort in old friends. So many countrymen from Russia came to sit with him and Aunt Zelda and Aunt Lena. Each night brought new people, new stories. Some had little to do with The Queen, but most had something to do with her. One night someone asked

Aunt Beast about her husband, Izzy, the painter. With that question a chilly silence descended.

That was the same night Pauline and her Russian had climbed up to The Queen's room to sit with us. They huddled quietly off to one side, listening to conversations. To break the awkwardness of the moment, Pauline's Russian rose and approached Papa. Papa and the Russian talked a long time. Papa called Uncle Meyer over to join in the conversation. I could tell Papa liked the Russian. Uncle Meyer, too. I didn't know how I felt about him.

Papa and Uncle Meyer and the Russian, they shook hands. Mama went over and hugged Pauline and drew her into the circle. But the newlyweds left a few minutes later.

I remembered my conversation in this very room with The Queen, how I'd confessed to loving Pauline, how I'd come to hate her in the end. I remembered The Queen's advice about falling in love. How could I have ever been in love with Pauline?

"Joseph, are you okay?"

Lizzie Kaplan was talking to me.

It turns out one of the people The Queen rescued from Russia was our real-estate agent, Lizzie Kaplan. She was one of the first The Queen brought to America after the immediate Michtom family. She must have been a little girl when The Queen rescued her, not much older than Emily.

"Joseph?"

I nodded, pulling myself together.

Lizzie Kaplan asked what grade I was in, what I thought about Papa and Mama's bears. She leaned close, listening to my answers, making me feel like I was the only person in the room. I never had anyone listen to me like that before.

NONE OF US could figure out how The Queen managed to bring a steady stream of countrymen to New York. But then, on the fifth night, The Queen's boss, Mr. Moscowitz from the raincoat factory, came to pay his respects. The raincoat factory boss, Mr. Moscowitz, you could tell right off he had a lot of feelings for The Queen. Such a short, fat man, as round as he was tall. We could have rolled him up and down Tompkins Avenue with just a push every now and then to keep him going. He had kinky, white hair. He wore a good black suit, and tons of cologne. He smelled like he just stepped out of the barbershop, though sweat beaded on his forehead and ran down the sides of his face. He didn't look so good, that Mr. Moscowitz. In fact, he looked like a man who had just lost his best friend. His eyes, red and puffy, gave away that maybe The Queen meant more to him than just a valued employee. He looked more like the grieving widower than a dutiful boss. I never saw a grown man sob before. But Mr. Moscowitz, after he'd been in The Queen's room ten minutes, suddenly broke down. He lowered his head, curled his back, and his body heaved. We all stared at him. Papa went over and sat by his side. He never said a word, Mr. Moscowitz, he just sobbed. And then he left.

Mama looked at Papa as the door closed behind him. Just a quick glance.

MR. MOSCOWITZ came only that once. But Lizzie Kaplan came every night.

Emily discovered that Lizzie Kaplan had danced professionally, a ballerina, until an injury ended that career. She'd gone into real estate at The Queen's suggestion. It had been a good decision.

On the seventh night, Lizzie Kaplan's profession in real estate became the topic of conversation in Tante Goldie's room. Aunt Beast, who had never heard of Lizzie Kaplan before this week, made a point of sitting beside her. Aunt Beast and Aunt Mouse had become home owners in the last week, thanks to The Queen. To make certain they always had a place to live, The Queen had bought each of them a property. Aunt Beast and Aunt Mouse never left the Lower East Side. But now they each owned an apartment house in Brooklyn.

"How could she buy us property in Brooklyn?" Aunt Beast asked. "She never crossed the bridge."

Gently, Lizzie Kaplan informed us that, in fact, Aunt Golda came to Brooklyn regularly. She'd passed our shop dozens of times. "How proud she was of you, Morris. May I call you Morris?"

Papa nodded.

"Why didn't she come in and say hello?" I asked.

"I guess your aunt Golda had her secrets," Papa said. "Most of them she took to the grave."

"I helped her choose these properties for you," Lizzie Kaplan told Aunt Beast and Aunt Mouse. "If you have any questions I hope you'll feel comfortable to ask me."

Aunt Beast had questions. "You think we should give up our flat on Henry Street?"

"Your sister thought it would be healthier if you did so," Lizzie Kaplan said.

"Healthier?"

"Less crowded, fresher air."

I understood why she would think that. The Queen's room felt like a steam bath.

"If my sister thought it was such an unhealthy neighborhood, why didn't *she* leave?" Aunt Beast asked.

"She liked this room, this building, and she liked being near her sisters."

"She said this?" Aunt Beast asked.

"She talked about moving to the country every now and then. But Golda was tired. Maybe she knew she wasn't well."

"This neighborhood she picked for us in Brooklyn, it's an up-and-coming?" asked Aunt Beast.

"I could take you there tomorrow," Lizzie Kaplan said. "You could see for yourself."

"Tomorrow?"

"This is the last night for sitting shivah. Is that correct, Morris?"

Papa nodded.

Lizzie Kaplan continued. "Golda hoped that if this day came I would be able to help you. It would be an honor to show you your properties."

Aunt Beast turned to Aunt Mouse. "Should we go look at real estate tomorrow?"

"I'll lose my job if I don't start sewing again, Zelda," Aunt Mouse said. "You will, too. As it is we can't pay the rent for August."

Papa took Aunt Mouse's hands in his own. "I can help you with your August rent, Lena. And you can always work for me. I could use both you and Zelda."

Lizzie Kaplan added, "Golda meant for you to give up the sewing someday, to become full-time businesswomen. I can manage the properties for you until you're ready. If that would help. But Golda believed the rent from the properties would be enough to support you. Perhaps even make you rich."

Aunt Beast perched on The Queen's best chair, between Lizzie Kaplan and Emily. The way she sat there, she reminded me of a vulture.

Emily leaned away from her, into my side. Even though under my three-piece suit sweat coated my skin, I put my arm around my sister and pulled her close.

The wonder of wonders in Luna Park will be the three-ringed mid-air circus, in which tight-rope walkers and lofty tumblers will do stunts without nets beneath them.

—THE NEW YORK TIMES

THE PARROT

Perhaps you think that under the bridge they would have no pets. What animal would stay with a band of lost children? But you would be wrong if you thought that. They had a parrot, a beautiful parrot, who came each night to roost with them, who spoke to them, though he often repeated himself.

What did the children care about that. The things he said set them rolling on the ground with glee. He had the foulest mouth of them all.

He had once belonged to a policeman and whenever he felt threatened he would scream,

STOP,

STOP,

STOP IN THE NAME OF THE LAW!

Those of guilty conscience, husbands on the lam, petty thieves, none ventured too near the children. Criminals only needed to hear the parrot's warning once. His booming voice sent the least and the worst offenders on their way. He sounded mighty, and mean.

And as the intruders' footsteps faded into the night the parrot would gossip with the children. Such naughty things he would say about all sorts of people who were even now sleeping in beds in fine houses.

But the parrot knew private things about them. Naughty, naughty things that made the children ache with laughter.

CHAPTER SEVEN

THERE HAD BEEN ILLNESS going around the neighborhood. Just in the week we sat shivah for The Queen, half the families on our block had someone down with the grippe. The famous Michtom luck had taken a wrong turn. Benjamin was sick, maybe he'd been infected by someone taking care of him. His cheeks burned like embers. His eyes and nose ran constantly, green stuff poured out, green the color of a bruise. His cough rattled us out of our sleep. How could such a little boy have such an evil cough?

"He needs to go to the hospital, Rose," Uncle Meyer said when he arrived for breakfast.

"No one can care for him better than I can," Mama said. "He'll get sicker at the hospital. You want he should get sicker? I know. I've seen it too many times. Babies get worse at the hospital. They get weaker and weaker and they die. Benjamin does not go to the hospital. It's bad enough we just lost Golda. We're not losing Benjamin, too. Do you hear me?"

"You're exhausted, Rose," Papa said. "Think of Joseph, think of Emily. You want they should take sick, too? And business . . . I can't run both the candy store and the bears without you."

"Joseph and Emily will help more, Morris. This is not up for discussion. Benjamin will not go to the hospital."

Mr. Kromer warmed up his clarinet on the sweltering corner.

"Maybe the nurse from school could come here," I suggested. "I bet she's got loads of free time in the summer."

"Joseph has a good idea. We'll get a nurse to come. You can live with that, Rose?" Uncle Meyer asked.

"Yes," Mama agreed. "A visiting nurse. Let *her* say if we need a hospital."

"YOUR BABY must be seen by a doctor immediately," the nurse said after examining Benjamin in the kitchen where Mama had moved his crib. The nurse, Miss Weil, looked so much like little Aunt Mouse that we all trusted her the minute she came through the door. "Benjamin is very sick, Mrs. Michtom."

"Can we fix him here at home, without the doctor?" Mama asked.

"You could care for him at home, certainly," the nurse

said. "But that may not be what's best for Benjamin. He needs a doctor's supervision. He needs constant care."

"I don't want a doctor," Mama said. "I don't want the hospital."

The nurse looked gently at Mama. "We can take him to a hospital where they don't care if you pay."

"You think I'm worried over money? Over money! You think I'd risk the life of my Benjamin over nickels and dimes?"

"Sometimes people can't afford the hospital. . . ."

"We can afford. We can afford," Mama said. "But two babies, they went last month to Brooklyn Hospital from this neighborhood. Two in one month. And neither of them came home. Instead two funerals we had."

"Maybe a different hospital, Mrs. Michtom. I could find a place for Benjamin at Memorial or Mount Sinai."

"You could stay here with me and help care for him. We would pay you. You be the doctor, Miss Weil. Would you do that?"

MAMA KNEW what she wanted. And she knew how to get it.

Miss Weil, when she went off her shift caring for Benjamin, rested on the couch, the one so recently vacated by Pauline Unger. Miss Weil and Mama took turns cooling Benjamin down, giving him medicine, spooning water between his peeling lips, changing his bedding. No matter what they did, Benjamin still lay like a lump and made the place stink of sickness; such a little kid, how could he fill the entire flat with such a stench? Mama and Miss Weil didn't seem to mind. But the sickroom odor did nothing for my appetite. I decided to eat with Uncle Meyer. I'd bring food wrapped in a napkin and we'd sit on the side of his bed, barefoot, in our shirtsleeves, and eat together. It turns out he couldn't stand watching Benjamin so sick, either.

"Miss Weil knows what she's doing. She shows Mama without saying Mama was maybe doing something wrong. They wash the screens with vinegar every hour or two. Makes me want to eat pickles all the time."

"You think your mama was doing something wrong?"

"No. Not wrong, Uncle Meyer. Not exactly wrong. Just not exactly right. Mama, you know how she can be. We don't see the same doctor two times in a row. But she likes Miss Weil. They can talk, you know, woman talk. Miss Weil just knows better how to help."

"And how is our Benjamin doing with such good care?" Uncle Meyer asked.

I don't know what it was about that question. I don't know but suddenly I got a vision of a world without Benjamin in it. It felt like I was being spun around in the water, dragged down. Like I was drowning.

I knew Benjamin wasn't dead. But suddenly I knew how it would feel if Benjamin did die. It felt different from losing The Queen. And that was bad enough.

I couldn't catch my breath. It felt like all the air in Uncle Meyer's room had been sucked out. I couldn't breathe.

Uncle Meyer saw I was in trouble. He stood up, motioned for me to put on my jacket, my socks and shoes, and follow him.

We walked.

To Prospect Park we walked. As the trolleys clanged past, as the horses jangled in their harnesses, as the carriages creaked and the automobiles sped by, we walked.

In Prospect Park, Uncle Meyer led me past the sheep, past the crowds of people, deeper and deeper, to a place I'd never been before. Deep inside the park the trees grew thick and close. The air no longer shimmered in the July heat. It was cool in there, and calm.

I heard it moments before I saw it. Where three paths came together we stopped.

Uncle Meyer had brought me to a small waterfall. It splashed into a fern-filled grotto. How many times had I been to Prospect Park? How many hours had I spent there? And this I'd never seen before.

Uncle Meyer rested his long fingers on my shoulders. "I come here sometimes. Not many people know about it. I trust you, Joe. You won't give away my secret, will you?"

I shook my head no.

We stood together for a long time, silent, watching the water spill over the rocks. I started to relax. It was the first time in a while that my ears had heard anything but the sound of Benjamin struggling for breath.

*   *   *

AS I NEARED home, I could hear Mr. Kromer's clarinet; I was thinking about Dilly's pickles. How much I wanted to share one with Benjamin. To see him reach out his hands and do the gimme, gimme and make the face like he always does when I give him a bite. With his eyes so big, and his grin spreading around the top and bottom of the pickle. It was just the thing on a summer afternoon. Maybe it was just the thing Benjamin needed to cure him.

Slowly I walked past Mr. Kromer, past the window of our shop. I climbed the stairs. Found Miss Weil in the kitchen. Asked if there was any change in Benjamin. But no, Miss Weil said, no, nothing new to report. Mama was sleeping. Backing out of the kitchen, I headed down to the street.

The front of the shop still resembled a candy store, though neighbors hardly ever dropped in anymore to make a purchase. Gus and Ira, they'd stopped coming months ago, not long after we got the letter from President Roosevelt.

I stood at the door. My eyes fixed on Papa's apron like I was hypnotized.

"You okay, Joseph?" Papa asked.

"Me, yeah. Sure. I'm fine, Papa. What do you want me to do?"

"Nothing. Go back out, Joseph. The way you look, you're not fit for inventory."

I didn't know how Papa and Emily could concentrate on

anything. Who could do inventory while Benjamin was so sick upstairs?

I STOOD on the corner, listening to Mr. Kromer and his clarinet. After a while I got up the nerve to interrupt. "Excuse me, Mr. Kromer. I'm sorry to bother you."

He took his clarinet from his lips and held it in front of him, waiting.

"Mr. Kromer, have you seen Dilly?"

"Dilly?" he said. "Dilly Lepkoff? The pickle man? Joseph, didn't you know? Dilly has a sick baby, too. He's been at home taking care of the other kids while the missus stays with the sick one in the hospital. Speaking of sick babies, how's little Benjamin doing?"

I knew with a queasy certainty. I knew without knowing how I knew. I knew there would be a funeral this week on Tompkins Avenue. Maybe it would be Dilly Lepkoff's baby. Maybe it would be ours. I didn't know which one it would be. But someone was going to die.

I felt like I was drowning again, the way it happened at Uncle Meyer's flat. But then it stopped. It was like, by taking me to the waterfall in Prospect Park, Uncle Meyer gave me a way to keep my head up and I could use it when I started going too deep.

Mr. Kromer stood looking at me, the fingers of his right hand running up and down his silent clarinet. He was waiting for an answer. I couldn't remember the question.

"Joseph, are you okay?"

"Yeah, Mr. Kromer."

"And Benjamin? He any better?"

"Benjamin's the same."

"It's a good thing you have the nurse to help."

"Yeah. A good thing."

He put his clarinet back to his lips.

"Mr. Kromer . . ."

The clarinet lowered.

"Yes, Joseph?"

I wanted to keep him talking. About anything. The Superbas. Coney Island. Anything. Anything to keep from being alone. But I could tell he was thinking more about the music and all the people who had passed in the last few minutes who had not dropped coins in his case.

"Never mind," I said. "Thanks."

I SLIPPED back inside the store. "Papa?"

Papa and Emily were marking down the candy. Papa knew his future wasn't made of sugar. It had fur, and button eyes, and stitched claws. Benjamin's illness, it forced Papa to choose. He was getting rid of the candy altogether and converting the entire shop to bear manufacturing until Lizzie Kaplan found the perfect location for a move. "Papa, did you know Dilly's baby is sick in the hospital? And Dilly's been home all week?"

"I heard," Papa said. "This is a bad summer for little

ones." He lifted his eyes to include Benjamin, fighting for his life above our heads, in the corner of our kitchen.

"Papa, if Dilly isn't selling pickles, how's he gonna pay his rent?"

Papa stopped. "Joseph, I . . ." He shut his mouth and tilted his head, studying me.

Emily sat down and pushed her dark hair back with a dusty hand.

"They must be hungry, Papa."

"Yes, Joseph. You're right."

Papa walked over to the cash register and opened the drawer. He took out three one-dollar bills. "Emily, get for your brother a bag of butterscotch."

"But Papa . . ."

"Do as I say."

Emily fetched the candy for me.

"Take these to Dilly," Papa said. "But don't overstay. You hear?"

Gus Lepkoff used to be my best friend. I knew how long to stay.

LEAVING THE LEPKOFFS' flat, slowly I climbed down their stairs and back onto the street. An automobile rattled past. The woman in the passenger seat laughed, her head thrown back. She clung to her enormous hat with both hands, trying to keep it on.

I didn't know how to tell Mama what I'd found at Dilly's.

His baby had been to the hospital. The hospital where babies are supposed to die. But now he was home. And he was better.

"The doctors say he should make a full recovery," Dilly said, his eyes shining. "I'll be back selling pickles tomorrow. Tell your papa I'll pay him what I owe him as soon as I can."

Dilly's kids, including the baby, were all well. They fell on the candy like they hadn't eaten in a month.

WHEN I GOT back home, I found Mama holding a limp Benjamin in her arms, wiping his body with a cool rag. Miss Weil was stripping off the bedclothes and remaking Benjamin's crib. She and Mama were one hundred percent in complete agreement about cleanliness in the sickroom, particularly when the sickroom also happened to be our kitchen.

"He was better a little earlier, Joseph," Mama said over Benjamin's head. "He even smiled. Didn't he, Lillian?"

Miss Weil nodded. But she kept her head down. I didn't like that. It could never be a good sign when grown-ups wouldn't look you in the eye. What did she know that she wasn't telling us?

I suspected I knew. It wasn't Dilly Lepkoff's family who was going to lose their baby. It was ours.

DICKIE TIDWELL

Dickie Tidwell took a shine to The Bride. Where she slept, he slept nearby, positioning his body between The Bride and the world outside, protecting her. He thought he could even protect her from the Radiant Boy, though he hoped he wouldn't have to.

Like a big dog, he followed her with his eyes, adoring, though he wouldn't touch her. And no one touched him. He was afraid of being touched, that Dickie Tidwell, who had once lived with his father, down cellar, in the servant's quarters of a fine house across from Prospect Park. He lived down cellar until the day young Dickie caught a robbery in progress. Three men in masks. And one his father. Dickie was blamed for letting in the thieves, which he never did. He never, never did. It was his father who let them in. An inside job.

His father hissed, I'll kill you, you little hoodlum. Double-cross your own flesh and blood? I'll lose everything because of you.

And Dickie's father meant what he'd said about killing Dickie. He beat Dickie Tidwell till his face swelled and his bones turned to splinters. But Dickie didn't die. He made his way, staggering and crawling through the night, the endless night, the night filled with raging pain. Dickie made his way to the children under the bridge.

His bleeding, bruised, and beaten self curled up in a corner watching, like a dog, wary like a dog, always guarding his back, his thoughts secret under heavy brows, scrappy, close to no one until The Bride came, the white-necked bride, who no longer wore her hair pinned up in the fashion of a lady, but down, in one thick braid, like a farm girl from Nebraska, like the mother he'd never had.

To keep the crowd on its feet, attractions beckon from one end of the park to the other. If someone should rest for more than a moment on a bench, a small band is dispatched to rouse the flagging guest.

—THE BROOKLYN DAILY EAGLE

CHAPTER EIGHT

I WONDERED IF I could find the falls myself. Without Uncle Meyer leading me.

The steamy summer day relaxed into evening. The sounds of Brooklyn spilled out of windows and doors.

From one backyard came singing. One whole block smelled of tomato sauce. People sat on chairs outside. They hung over windowsills. They called to each other from rooftops and fire escapes.

"Hey Joe, wanna get a game up?" That was Ira Gershowitz.

"Not tonight, Ira," I called back. "Thanks anyway."

"Yeah. Sure."

I could hear that edge to his voice. Like maybe he thought I thought I was too good to play ball with the likes of him.

I wish I could have just settled into a game with Ira, with

Gus, with the guys. But all I could think about was Benjamin. So I kept moving.

PLENTY OF people had come to Prospect Park that summer evening to cool off. Kids slept on sheets spread out on the grass. Every one of those kids was going to live through the night and wake up tomorrow and shout and laugh and race across the park and annoy their families. Some of the kids had bears. Our bears. One little girl slept with a bear cradled in her arms. Another, sucking her thumb, had wrapped her bear in a doll blanket beside her.

I wandered in the twilight. Everything looked so different. A street kid brushed past, his feet filthy, his red hair poking out from under a dark cap. He wore short pants held up by a rope belt. The pants were shredded like something had been eating the hems. I adjusted my gray cap and kept walking.

I wanted to find the falls myself. I needed to find the falls myself. But after searching awhile I gave up. Maybe Uncle Meyer was some sort of Harry Houdini, some kind of magician who could make me believe in something that wasn't real. Maybe there never was a waterfall. It was all an illusion.

OUR EMPTY SHOP shone like a jewel on Tompkins Avenue, the only place on the whole block all lit up. Why hadn't Papa and Emily turned down the lights when they'd finished? My mind jumped to the only possible answer. Something had happened to Benjamin. I stood on the street, unable to make myself move.

Miss Weil met me at the bottom of the stairs. Someone must have seen me and sent her down.

Gently, she took my hand and squeezed it. She led me up the steps to our flat. I dreaded what I would find when we came through the kitchen door. This was it. My brother was gone. He'd died without ever playing street ball, or falling in love. He'd died without ever going to Coney Island.

But at the top of the stairs the door creaked open and sitting in Papa's lap was Benjamin, a very alive Benjamin, eating bits of boiled chicken off a small china plate.

He looked up at me and smiled before he went back to eating.

Mama stood at the window, facing the street. She glanced at me when I entered the kitchen and her eyes told me everything I needed to know. That Benjamin had turned the corner. That he would be fine. Just like the Lepkoffs' baby. He would be fine.

"About two hours ago," Miss Weil said. "The fever broke. Benjamin pointed to his bear and told your mama they were both hungry."

"There. You see? I knew he shouldn't go to the hospital," Mama said, facing us.

No funerals this week on Tompkins Avenue after all. I rubbed my hand over my eyes.

"He keeps asking for pickles," Papa said. "Isn't that something?"

"Tomorrow, Benjamin, we will share one of Dilly's pickles," I said.

"Morris," Mama said. "Someone should tell Meyer that Benjamin's okay."

"You got enough snap left, Joseph, to run to Fulton?" Papa asked.

"Sure," I said. "I'll go."

Emily put her hand in mine. "I'll go with you."

Mr. Kromer had already left for the day. "I'll tell him Benjamin's okay tomorrow, first thing."

"You know," Emily said, struggling to keep up with me. "They came around collecting for Dilly two days ago. Papa gave them money enough for rent and food and a little extra. Papa said Dilly'll probably use the money you brought today to pay doctor bills."

I wanted with all my heart to tell Emily about the waterfall. I wanted to take her, I wanted to take Benjamin. I knew it was Uncle Meyer's secret place. But some secrets shouldn't be kept. Not from your sister and brother. I'd tell them. I'd take them. I remembered now. I remembered exactly how Uncle Meyer led me there. I'd show them as soon as Mama let us take Benjamin out again.

But first, I had to have a moment alone with Uncle Meyer.

HELEN AND NINA

Helen and Nina had been raised as sisters by mistake. Two babies had been born on the same night, in the same hospital, on the same ward. One belonging to Helen's mother, one belonging to a Mrs. Adler. A nurse mixed up the babies. She gave Helen's real sister to Mrs. Adler. Mrs. Adler's baby squirmed in Helen's mother's arms. Neither mother spoke English. Neither could make her protests understood.

When Helen's mother brought little Nina home, Helen's father left. He said the baby wasn't his. And Helen's mother beat her chest because she knew he was right. The hospital made her take a stranger's child. Helen's mother thought, if they would not let her have her own baby, this America, this strange and frightening America, at least they gave her a baby, some baby, any baby. But though she tried, she could not love this baby who was not her flesh and blood. She was absent more and more from Helen's and Nina's lives.

But Helen loved Nina. She cared for her. Fed her. Bathed her.

When the mistake was finally made right, the Adler parents, Nina's real parents, had already died in a trolley accident. The child with them, Helen's flesh-and-blood sister, though bruised, was going to survive.

The ambulance arrived at the very hospital where the mistake had been made three years earlier and the nurse remembered that night and the names of the two baby girls. For three years she had carried this burden and she knew finally she had a chance to make good, at least for those who still survived. So she contacted Helen's mother and just like that, Helen's mother was given her own flesh and blood, but Helen couldn't surrender, wouldn't surrender Nina, who was her sister regardless of what anyone said.

And so she stole her, a terrible thing. But who would have loved Nina if Helen hadn't taken her? What orphanage could have loved her as much? No one, no, no one loved Nina the way Helen loved her. So she took her to live under the bridge. And sometimes she worried if she'd done the right thing. But most of the time she was certain she had.

CHAPTER NINE

LIZZIE KAPLAN'S FIRST MISTAKE was thinking Aunt Zelda and Aunt Lena were anything like The Queen. Neither of them took to the job of landlady. Aunt Beast preferred her flat on Henry Street and didn't want to move to the outskirts of Brooklyn, in spite of a sudden, nasty invasion of bugs throughout the Lower East Side. Bugs everywhere, they hid in the bedding, in drawers, in plumbing fixtures.

Aunt Beast was lucky. The bugs had not made their way to her property in Brooklyn, but if they had, she knew the tenants would yammer at her the way she was yammering at her Henry Street landlord to get rid of the infestation. Aunt Beast liked the *idea* of owning property. But she didn't like the responsibility of caring for it.

Aunt Mouse, too, felt overwhelmed by the tasks of owning a building. She took everything to heart. She tried, herself, to solve the bug problem in their flat on Henry Street so that she'd be prepared when the bugs reached her Brooklyn property, but the pesky insects resisted every effort.

THE FIRST MONTH of my aunts as property owners had not quite ended before they called a meeting with Lizzie Kaplan at our flat on Tompkins Avenue. Hah. What would The Queen say about that? Finally, her sisters had crossed the Brooklyn Bridge.

The sound of Mr. Kromer's clarinet floated in through the open kitchen windows.

Children passing below shouted at one another in a mock fight.

All the Michtom relations settled around the table.

Mama had stacked bear parts and paperwork on the couch in an effort to make our flat more presentable. Little difference that made. But no one, not even Aunt Beast, commented on our messy kitchen. They talked instead about the weather and the neighbors.

Out of the blue Aunt Mouse lifted a spoon and tapped it gently against her teacup. "I have an announcement," she said.

When she was certain she had everyone's attention, in a quavering voice Aunt Mouse said, "I'm leaving."

Papa stood, came over to his sister, put his hands on her small shoulders. "Shah, shah, Lena. It's been a hard month. We're still getting over losing Golda."

"No, Morris." Now her voice sounded a little stronger. "I'm certain. I'm leaving. One of my tenants, she knows someone in the Jewish Removal Society and they need a representative to travel around the country finding towns where Jews would be welcome."

"Jewish Removal Society?" Papa said. "That doesn't sound like a very honorable group."

"But they are, Morris," Aunt Mouse said. "They're trying to relieve the crowding on the Lower East Side. If not, the government will start sending people back to the hell they came from. This is the only chance they have."

"You'll save people, like Tante Goldie," Emily said, her latest book, *Pinocchio,* closed and resting in her lap.

"Yes," Aunt Mouse said. "Yes, *mamaleh,* a little like Tante Golda. She helped bring people here. I'll help keep them here. Get them good jobs, good homes, make certain the door to America stays open. You see, I always wanted to travel."

"I never knew," Papa said.

Aunt Beast nodded. "Oh, yes. She loved it. When we made the crossing she was the only one who didn't turn green."

"But who will look after your property?" Mama asked. "And how will you support yourself?"

Benjamin had crept into Aunt Mouse's lap and she stroked his curly head. "The Removal Society pays a fair wage."

"You already have the job?" Aunt Beast asked. Up until now she had been only half listening, as if this was just another of Aunt Mouse's silly ideas. Now, suddenly, Aunt Lena had her full attention.

"They offered the job to me today," Aunt Lena said.

"And you will take it? You will leave me?"

Aunt Lena touched Aunt Zelda's arm. "Think how much better that flat will be if you're not sharing it. Golda discovered benefits from living alone, yes?"

"God forbid I should have such 'benefits.'"

Mama and Papa exchanged that glance again, the one they exchanged after Mr. Moscowitz, the raincoat man, left The Queen's room during our week of mourning.

Aunt Lena had something more to say.

"As for my property, Rose is correct. I need someone to take it over."

"And?" Aunt Beast said. "What are you getting at, Lena?"

"Maybe Miss Kaplan should explain."

"Your sister," Lizzie Kaplan said to Aunt Beast, "would like to sell her property to you."

"To me?" Aunt Beast looked dumbstruck. "I don't like managing the property I already own. Why would I want two?"

"From the time these properties were purchased until this day," Lizzie Kaplan explained, "their value has doubled. People are moving across the bridge. The part you enjoy, Zelda, if I'm not mistaken, is owning the property. I suspect you will enjoy even more the buying and selling of it. You already own one. Your sister would like to sell you hers. You, then, can turn around and sell them both and buy a bigger property, a better one. Or several new ones. Do you understand?"

Aunt Beast poked a finger at Aunt Mouse. "Where would I find the money to pay for your building?"

Aunt Lena smiled sweetly. "Oh, Zelda. I'm certain we can work something out."

AFTER AUNT ZELDA and Aunt Lena returned to Manhattan to further discuss Aunt Lena's plans, Lizzie Kaplan remained in our kitchen.

Mama put Benjamin to bed but she let me and Emily climb out on the fire escape. We scaled the two flights and sat under the stars, outside the top-floor flat, our legs dangling through the metal rail, listening, watching Brooklyn.

"Will we ever see Aunt Mouse again?" Emily asked.

"She'll come back. She'll miss Aunt Beast bossing her around. You'll see."

"We should have a going-away party for her," Emily said.

"On Coney Island," I added.

Emily agreed. "On Coney Island."

"We could go to the moon . . ."

"And ride the chutes . . ."

"And see the wild animals . . ."

"And the tiny, tiny babies . . ."

I had no interest in the incubator babies but I went along with Emily anyway.

We started back down the fire escape, quietly, so as not to disturb the neighbors on the third floor. We couldn't wait to share our idea of Aunt Mouse's going-away party with Mama and Papa.

The serious tone in the kitchen stopped us. Emily and I

huddled together on the landing outside the window, out of sight, listening.

Lizzie Kaplan spoke so softly we didn't dare move for fear of missing a word.

"She saved my life," Lizzie said and we knew "she" could only mean The Queen. "Twice your Golda saved my life. The first time I was nearly Joseph's age when a Cossack had his way with me. First he tied up my parents. Then he did this thing to me right in front of them. He murdered my parents. He thought he had killed me, too. He was drunk. He left our house, set it on fire. I managed to get out, to crawl to a neighbor. Your sister heard of my story and she got me out of Russia. But when I came here I had nothing. I was broken in a way that doctors couldn't fix. That is when your sister saved my life a second time. She became my family. She was so good to me, your Golda, I would do anything to honor the memory of your sister."

Mama asked, "Do you have anyone now, Lizzie?"

"No," Lizzie Kaplan said, "after all these years, no."

Though I couldn't see her, I imagined her at the table, flanked by Mama and Papa, amid all the pieces of unassembled bears, her back dancer-straight in her shirtwaist, her dark hair a crown on her head.

"While your sister lived I needed no one else. She was my mother, my sister, my friend."

"Then we must be that for each other," Mama said.

It grew quiet in the kitchen.

I looked at my sister, Emily, in the moonlight. She reached out her small hand and I took it. I would never let anything like what happened to Lizzie Kaplan happen to Emily. I'd die first.

We gave Mama, Papa, and Lizzie a few minutes more before we emerged from the fire escape, into the kitchen. We said nothing about Coney Island.

THE NEXT DAY, Papa set The Queen's document box in a place of honor on the big oak bookcase in the living room. All papers and bear parts were cleared away at least from that one shelf. The Queen's box held all the receipts, all the promises of a new life for dozens of people, including a yellowing one with Lizzie Kaplan's name on it.

Later that day Papa hung on the wall a beautiful frame in which was a piece of paper printed nicely in good ink. It was The Queen's citizenship paper in my careful script. Papa hung it on the living room wall between his and Mama's citizenship papers, right along with the letter from President Roosevelt.

CHAPTER TEN

LIZZIE KAPLAN BECAME a regular at the round oak table in the kitchen. Unlike when Pauline lived with us, this time Uncle Meyer didn't stay away. The first night we all gathered in the kitchen on Tompkins Avenue he and Lizzie sat across from each other, divided by Mama and Emily on one side, me and Papa on the other. Benjamin ate early and sat on the kitchen floor, playing with his bear, while the rest of us had our meal.

Lizzie Kaplan asked Mama and Papa about the bear business, she asked Emily about the book she was reading. When addressed, Lizzie talked about Aunt Zelda's emerging skills in real estate.

In the beginning she was quiet at the table, respectful, attentive. She listened to everyone, her head turning from speaker to speaker, her eyes bright with interest. By dessert the first night, Uncle Meyer got us onto the subject of politics.

Lizzie Kaplan seemed reluctant to voice an opinion. She talked instead about opera.

"You like opera?" Uncle Meyer asked.

It turns out they saw the same performances.

"Funny," Uncle Meyer said, "how you can keep crossing paths with someone and never notice."

AFTER THAT I traded seats with Lizzie Kaplan and she sat next to Uncle Meyer. By the third night Lizzie no longer needed prompting. She contributed to the noise at the table along with everyone else.

With a rowdy crowd filling our kitchen again, Mama's food tasted better. She remembered how to laugh. So did Papa.

Uncle Meyer learned that Lizzie loved anything with coconut.

"Rose, let me contribute dessert tomorrow," he told my mother, his arm resting gently on Mama's shoulder.

And the next night he brought coconut cake. Coconut cake he'd made with his own two hands. Who knew Uncle Meyer could bake? I thought that's why he ate with us all the time. It turns out my uncle with the banana fingers knew more than a little about working in a kitchen.

Mama beamed at her brother. She watered the friendship between Lizzie Kaplan and Uncle Meyer like it was a fancy hothouse plant.

Our kitchen shook again with loud, passionate discussions

and it almost felt like old times when Mama and Papa had an interest in something other than bears. We fell in love with Lizzie Kaplan. She made us a family again in a way we hadn't been since President Roosevelt went to Mississippi.

Pauline Unger also helped in her own way by bringing us her Russian, who Papa hired to oversee the cutters. After only weeks on the job Pauline's Russian already lightened some of the load on Papa's shoulders. Not enough to take a night off and go to Coney Island. But enough that Papa and I stopped fighting.

Well, we didn't fight as much.

There is the "leap-frog railway," which is also over the sea. . . .
Two cars running on the same track meet head-on in hair-
raising fashion. But instead of telescoping, as they do in
railway collisions on land, the cars slide over each other
in loop-the-loop style, and continue their journey.

—THE NEW YORK TIMES

MAY

The Radiant Boy moved in and out of their nights under the bridge. No one envied him, so smooth on his feet, waves of chill rolling off him. The Radiant Boy was definitely dead. But sometimes the children under the bridge weren't certain. That's how they felt about May, the girl with the black mouth, her lips burned by carbolic acid, her arms lined with fine cuts. She wore all white like the Radiant Boy and some of the children said,

That's how you tell—if they wear white, they're dead for sure.

But what if someone just likes to wear white?

May's face was a bad deal even before the poison. It refused to arrange itself into anything pleasant. She looked like a girl who might wish never to see her own reflection. She didn't talk to them and some of the children said,

That's how you tell, if they don't talk.

But what if the poison burned her voice?

She just cried. Silent tears rolling down her cheeks, her eyes two green bruises in a dusky face. The tears made snail trails down her skin and the burns around her mouth oozed.

If you tried to look her in the eye, she turned away.

But she didn't want to be alone. She kept seeking them out, pushing near them like the runt of the litter, whose brothers and sisters despise it, whose mother ignores it, yet it pushes back and squirms into the inner circle. She wanted to be part of the giant whelping box under the bridge, of its warmth and its smell. And the children under the bridge even if they didn't know, dead or alive, let the girl, May, stay. They didn't feed her because they didn't know if she ate. Her mouth, with those sores, how could she eat? But once The Bride touched May's cheek, and May let her, but only once. And The Bride said,

Alive. Her cheek is warm.

If The Bride said "alive" then most of the children believed, especially Dickie. But not everyone. And the ones who thought,

Dead,

no matter how she tried to get close to them, they kept their distance.

OTTO

The children under the bridge became family to one an-
other when their own families had no room for them, or no
interest, or had come undone. Sometimes they stuck up for
one another. Sometimes they fought with one another.
Just like any family. But even the least popular child un-
der the bridge belonged. And when he suffered, the re-
venge of the bridge children came swift and sure.

The children were sorely tested by Otto, who could
not remember any other life but the one he lived with the
hermit of Inwood, Otto's great-grandfather.

Otto stayed with the old man's body for three days
after he'd died, freezing in their hut, afraid to leave the
old man's side, hoping he'd open his eyes and say,

Had you fooled that time, didn't I?

But eventually the boy understood that the tiny hut
on the meadow would never be warm again unless he set it
on fire, which he did, before he wandered away and found
a new life under the bridge.

Otto loved setting fires. The children let him light the
ash can stove at night, the stove that kept them warm un-
der the bridge. During the day Otto followed fire trucks,
racing behind them through Brooklyn. He boasted about
the uniform he would wear one day. He would sleep in the
firehouse and ride the clanging trucks. He couldn't tell the

difference between people who started fires and people who put them out. It was all fire to Otto.

But one late afternoon, caught by a group of thugs, Otto was dragged behind a firehouse, stripped of his clothes. Otto was tough, but he was outnumbered and outsized. They stuffed a gag in his mouth and dodged his kicks and punches as best they could. They pushed him, naked, into the firehouse basement. He fought with a fury they'd never expected. He frightened them and that made them crueler. The thugs covered Otto's bare skin in red paint. Then they tied him up and left him in the dark. When Otto managed to escape, he flew back to the bridge, wild with anger, naked but for the layer of paint. The children under the bridge learned as he hissed and spit out his tale, they learned what had befallen him and The Bride and Helen tried bathing him in the East River, trying to wash off the heavy layer of paint, but he shook them off, a rabid dog, furious at the sympathy of girls. So Max and Karl scrubbed Otto instead, roughly, until Otto was raw. And when Max and Karl left the bridge the next morning, they headed to the neighborhood where Otto had been shamed. They waited, watching until they caught two boys red-handed, one of them wearing Otto's black stiff hat, the hat that had once belonged to the old hermit.

When they came back that evening they carried two sets of clothes. They put Otto's hat back on his head.

We didn't leave them with even a coat of paint,

and Otto grinned, imagining two of his attackers trapped on the streets of Brooklyn, naked as shaved cats. And how would they explain that to their fathers?

Otto gloated. Otto, who did not have to explain himself to anyone.

Karl gave Otto his choice of the two suits, nice suits, hardly any holes anywhere. And he had shoes with laces for the first time he could ever remember, though everything was twice too big. Otto looked up, his mouth twitching with a hint of cruel pleasure, his skin still tinted pink. It made Otto look fierce, even fiercer than he normally looked.

But when Karl offered Otto the match to light the ash can stove that night, Otto said,

Nah,

and walked away.

There is a large arena in which the spectators may watch a whole city block burn down, with thrilling rescues from factory windows, real fire engines, and all that sort of thing.

—THE NEW YORK TIMES

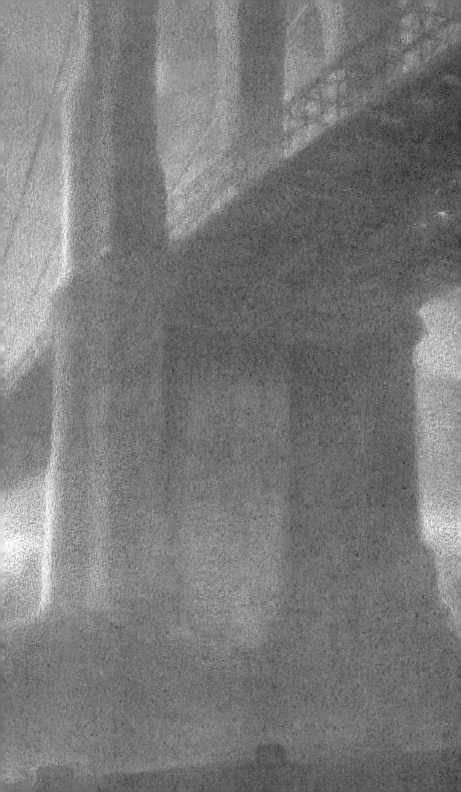

AUGUST 1903

CHAPTER ELEVEN

MOST EVENINGS GUYS SHOWED UP on the street, hoping for a game of stickball.

The same guys every night, Al, Frank, Mike, Lenny, Mitch, Gus, George, Ira.

On Hancock, with its first- and second-floor bays, the Rostowsky family followed our games from their big front window.

Nobody kept secrets in our corner of Brooklyn. Everyone knew the Rostowskys. They'd been attacked in their village in Russia years ago. One of the Rostowsky boys, the oldest, Samuel, died from the beating the Cossacks gave him. The other, Jacob, was only four, not much older than Benjamin is now. In that same attack, Jacob had his head smashed in by the butt of a rifle. Even though he survived, Jacob never learned how to act right.

Mr. and Mrs. Rostowsky protected Jacob. You can't blame

them, really. Jacob had been a smart kid in the Old Country. Mrs. Rostowsky told Mama that at four he could already read. He talked all the time, she said. Now instead of being the smartest kid on the block he couldn't remember from one time to the next how to tie his own shoes.

Jacob wouldn't be going back to school with the rest of us next month. He'd been in our class for a few years but not anymore. Jacob didn't understand geography or history. How could he? You could tell him something ten times and he'd still ask you about it the eleventh like the subject had never come up before.

We didn't ask him to play ball with us. He looked like one of us, but he couldn't even walk straight, how could he hit a ball?

The Rostowsky family loved baseball as much as the rest of us. Maybe even a little more. They took Jacob to almost every Superbas game at Washington Park. Mr. Rostowsky painted signs for a living. He had a good business. I guess you could say the Rostowskys, like the Michtoms, had gotten lucky. They, too, had found their land of gold.

And it seemed like their favorite part of that golden land was baseball. If you asked Jacob what he wanted to do when he grew up, he said he wanted to play for the Superbas. The truth is, Jacob had never even held a bat. Probably never would.

THE SUPERBAS weren't having a great year. Over the last two seasons they'd lost most of their best players. They still had Jack Doyle, but you couldn't count on Dirty Jack. He'd be the big hero one game, a big bum the next. That didn't matter to the Rostowskys. They bought their season tickets, sat in the outfield, and cheered the home team no matter how badly they played.

From time to time the Rostowskys invited one of us kids to go along with them so Jacob could have a friend. We never turned them down. What guy would miss a chance to go to a game at Washington Park? But it was hard not to be embarrassed by Jacob who, when he got excited, made weird noises. People turned and stared.

One night, we were just about to get a game going when Jacob teetered over to me.

"You wanna come see the Superbas, Joe?" Jacob asked, his parents flanking him, just in case he couldn't get the words out right.

Seeing his parents there annoyed me. I thought how much I wanted to go to a Superbas game with my own parents. Or even more, to Coney Island. But Jacob's offer was something real, and it was too good to refuse.

"Sure, Jake," I said. "A game would be great."

"You wanna come to the game, Joe?" Jacob asked again.

I looked to his parents for guidance. They didn't take their eyes off Jacob.

"I'd really like that, Jake. Sure."

"Sure," Jacob said. "Joe said, 'sure.'"

Mr. and Mrs. Rostowsky smiled.

"You wanna come to a game, Joe?" Jacob turned and asked again.

Emily appeared at my elbow. "Hi, Jake. Hi, Mrs. Rostowsky, Mr. Rostowsky. Joe, Mama says to come home."

"Joe's coming to a game with me," Jacob told Emily.

"Lucky Joe," Emily said, smiling.

I tugged on the visor of the genuine Superbas baseball cap Jacob always wore, a cap his parents had gotten for him, I don't know how. "We're gonna have a good time, Jake."

"We're gonna have a good time," Jacob echoed.

Mrs. Rostowsky took Jacob's hand and led him back inside their apartment.

"We're gonna have a good time," he said, in that voice that was just a little too loud, a little too strained, as the door closed behind him.

CHAPTER TWELVE

"JOE'S GOING WITH THE ROSTOWSKYS to see the Super-bas," Emily informed Mama and Papa as we came through the door into the kitchen.

"That's nice," Mama said. "Jacob doesn't have many friends, poor boy."

"I'm not Jacob Rostowsky's friend, Mama. I'm just going to a baseball game with his family. They asked. I said yes. No big deal."

"You be nice to that boy," Mama said.

"What do you think I'd be, Mama?"

"Joseph, you don't know how lucky you are."

"I know, I know. How can I forget with everybody telling me all the time?"

Mama said, "Some of the boys take advantage of Jacob. Some boys, they're not nice. Someone stole his home run ball. That's like stealing a letter from President Roosevelt. Who would do such a thing? The boy's been through enough already."

"I'll be nice, Mama. Don't worry."

Mama nodded. She pointed me in the direction of the latest arrival of bears, boxes and boxes of them to be inspected, sorted, repacked. She returned to her paperwork. Papa and Uncle Meyer pored over contracts at the table.

If I had a choice, I hoped the Rostowskys would take me to see the Superbas play the Pirates. Now that would be a good game.

"Hey, Joe, you think you can sneak me into Washington Park when you go?"

I looked up at Emily. As far as I could tell, my sister didn't know a bunt from a box score. She didn't care about baseball. All she really cared about was reading. But she hated to miss out on anything. And she especially hated it when I got to do something she couldn't do.

"You know I can't get you in, Em. I'll be with the Rostowskys."

"It won't be that great anyway. The Superbas stink this year."

I snorted. I'd said those exact words to her a dozen times already this season, but it still sounded funny coming out of her mouth.

"Emily, *mamaleh*, someday we'll go to a baseball game," Mama said.

"Yeah," I sniped. "Like someday we'll go to Coney Island."

Mama gave me the eyebrow.

I DIDN'T MIND so much about sitting with Jacob if the game really turned out good. Even though he was Jacob, he'd been there in 1900 when the Superbas took the pennant. Everyone who saw that game, I mean everyone, they'd seen the best. No one could take that away.

Only that was three years ago, and Jacob was still loud, strange, brain-bashed Jacob.

WILLIE

The doctors said about Willie that he wasn't all there. His father hated the sight of him and kept him locked in a room with a rag tied over his mouth to keep him quiet. The day he escaped he unknotted the rag and tied it around his neck. He never took it off, never, because what Willie remembered about that rag was not his father. What Willie remembered was his mother, gently wiping his face with it.

The kids under the bridge didn't mind the way Willie was. He didn't seem that different to them except that maybe he did whatever they asked without question. Whatever they asked. He never complained.

And he was the best at bringing in money of all of them.

CHAPTER THIRTEEN

I ENDED UP GETTING MY WISH for a Pirates game. Pittsburgh was playing the Superbas in Brooklyn three days in a row. The Rostowskys asked if I'd like to come see the final match.

The first two days the Superbas had lost; the Pirates wiped the floor with us. I could only hope we'd do better today. At least we had good weather. Not too hot. No rain for a change. Just a little breeze. And the sky that clean summer blue. A perfect day for baseball.

I took a bath the night before and Mama insisted I wear a new union suit. She laid out my double-breasted summer coat and matching pants. Dressy. But not so dressy the clothes would call attention to me.

I burst out of the store onto the crowded sidewalk, squinting at the sun. Mr. Kromer occupied his usual spot on the corner; he and his clarinet kept people and traffic moving.

Mama had given me a little money so I could pay for my ticket or, if the Rostowskys wouldn't accept that, at least pay for my own food. Everybody gets hungry at Washington Park. It smells like fried onions and Red Hots and popcorn. How could you not get hungry?

I passed Dilly on my way to the Rostowskys and bought a good luck pickle. My mouth swam just watching him lift a big, fat one out of the barrel and wrap it in paper. I ate the pickle leaning forward so the juice didn't run down my arm and make my clothes stink of vinegar. Savoring the burn at the back of my throat, I crunched through the pickle skin into the juicy middle, bite after bite. By the time I reached the Rostowskys the last bit of pickle slid down my throat. Inside my cheeks tingled. My tongue felt as happy as Mr. Kromer's clarinet. Like I had swallowed summer.

Jacob, in a school suit, waited in the front hall. The Rostowskys kept a little bench there. "I'm sick, Joe."

My heart sank.

My mouth still felt all sassy with pickle juice, but my heart sank.

"I'm sick, Joe. I threw up."

There were a number of reasons why I didn't want to hear any more on the subject. But Jake didn't care.

"I got sick, Joe," Jake repeated. "I'm so excited."

"Getting excited can make you sick all right, Jake."

"I got excited about the game."

"I'm pretty excited, too," I said.

"Did you get sick, Joe?"

Mrs. Rostowsky came into the front hall. She put her hand across Jacob's forehead and stood with her head cocked, like she was listening to the inside of his head through her hand. Like the inside of Jacob's head was telling her how it felt.

Mrs. Rostowsky looked over at me. "You look so nice, Joe. Are you ready?"

I nodded.

"Joe's excited, too," Jacob said.

We walked to the trolley stop and waited, but not for long. Mr. Rostowsky had the trolley schedule down to a science. The car pulled up, packed. No one got off. Jacob and I had to stand and hang on to the straps.

"It's crowded," Jacob said.

I don't know why his stating the obvious annoyed me so much.

I pressed against the people behind me in order to put a little distance between me and the Rostowskys.

"I feel sick," Jacob said.

That got Mr. and Mrs. Rostowsky's attention.

"I feel sick," Jacob repeated. In fact, Jacob had the attention of everyone on the trolley car.

Passengers squeezed toward the other end of the car, giving us more room than I imagined possible in such a crowd.

"I feel sick. Oh, I feel sick."

People actually got off at the next stop and said they'd wait for another car.

Our end of the trolley emptied. Jacob and I sat down. It felt like we had our own private streetcars.

"It's less crowded now. You feel any better, Jake?" I asked.

Jacob smiled. "I didn't really feel sick, Joe."

My grin mirrored the grin on Jacob's face.

"You're okay, Jake, you know."

"I'm okay, Joe."

I TOOK MY money to the concession and bought two Red Hots. One for me, one for Jake.

"You like mustard, relish, onions?" I asked.

"The works, Joe."

"You're a good boy, Joseph Michtom," Mrs. Rostowsky whispered into my ear.

That took care of all the money Mama had given me but it spread out the whole going-to-the-game feeling in a real nice way. And it kept Jake quiet a long time. Jake was a very slow eater.

"I'm glad you came with us, Joe," Jacob said as we sat, waiting for the game to start.

"Yeah, me, too."

The ballpark was full. I couldn't have snuck anyone in even if I'd tried.

In the sunlight I could see Jacob had a shadow over his upper lip. A mustache. He'd need to start shaving soon. Would Jacob ever be able to shave himself?

Jacob should have made girls crazy to go out with him.

But no one, not one girl, ever did anything nice for Jacob, never gave him anything, never even stopped to talk with him, never touched his sleeve the way some of them do. Not one girl. Except Emily.

If the Russians hadn't bashed in his head when he was four, Jake'd be maybe the most popular guy at school. Now he wasn't even going to school.

The game started and it was clear from the first inning that we were going to get our money's worth. The Pirates acted all cocky after slaughtering us two days in a row. But today the Superbas weren't having any of it.

Jake watched the game like if he missed one play he'd get thrown into a den of lions or something. I thought he'd be talking all the time but he never said a word. Until we brought in our first run. Superbas, one. Pirates, zero. Jake went crazy then. But everyone else in the park went crazy then, too.

We got one more run off of them that afternoon.

They got nothing off us.

We shut them out.

ON THE WAY home the entire trolley full of people celebrated. And our trolley was just one little pip of excitement spreading out from Washington Park to every corner of Brooklyn.

I thanked the Rostowskys for taking me and headed back down Hancock. Instantly, the guys crowded around. They wanted the details of the game. Jake watched from his stoop while I got all the attention.

"I need to get home," I said, uncomfortable.

But I agreed to come back after dinner. For a game of stickball.

I WASN'T SURE Mama and Papa would let me go. I hadn't done any work all day. And now I wanted to play ball tonight.

"Go," Papa said. "You're fourteen years old. We can afford to give you a day off."

"He's had enough time off," Mama said. "We'll never fill these orders without him, Morris."

"We'll fill them. Don't fret, Rose. It'll make you old. Go, Joseph," Papa said. "Just don't break any windows."

Al had done that last month. He'd be working off what he owed the rest of the summer.

Before I left the house, I changed out of my good suit.

The sun, still high, bounced off the brick and cement of Brooklyn, filling the street with summer light.

Chapter Fourteen

THE MINUTE IRA AND GEORGE arrived with the broom-stick we chose up sides.

My team played like the Superbas on a bad day. By the time we came up to bat in the last inning, we trailed by six runs and it was getting dark. That's when Jacob stepped out of his house. I only noticed because usually Jake stayed in and watched us from the window. He never came out to watch.

But I was wrong about him. He hadn't come out to watch. He'd come out to play.

"Joe," he said. "Can I be on your team?"

The guys looked at each other. Only Mitch started to laugh but it came out sounding like a cough. Both sides turned to me.

We were so far behind, in no way could our team win. I looked at the guys, all of them. And they looked back. They were leaving it up to me.

I sighed, raised one eyebrow. A nod started with me and moved all the way around the circle. I kicked a stone into the gutter. Then I looked back at Jacob.

"Yeah," I said, nodding. "You're just in time. Go sit and wait. I'll call you when it's your turn at bat."

We had two outs already. The way we were playing, short of a miracle, we'd be out, it'd be dark, and the game would be over before the lineup ever opened with a spot for Jake.

Ira was up next. He popped it. It could have been an easy out. Game over. But Lenny, the outfielder for the other team, standing halfway down Hancock Street, he let the ball go. He was right there but he let the ball go and suddenly we had a guy on base.

So now we've got Ira on first and Al gets up. Al's totally unpredictable. Sometimes he connects the bat to the ball and gets himself a home run. Sometimes he strikes out in three swings.

His first two swings went wild. But I swear on the third pitch Frank slowed down and aimed for Al's bat. He tipped a ground ball on the pitch. Now we had Ira on second, Al on first, and Gus was up.

Gus, a pretty solid hitter, was last in the batting lineup before Jake. I couldn't believe what was happening. What the guys were doing.

"Warm yourself up, Jake," I said. "You're up next."

The pitcher threw so crazy, Gus never got a chance to swing. They walked him.

Now the bases were loaded.

And Jake came up to bat.

FRANK TOSSED the ball at Jake the way I toss a ball for Benjamin. Nice and easy.

Jake. He was excited. He swung the stick so hard it flew out of his hands, landing with a clatter across the street. The ball went straight to the catcher.

Second pitch. Jake spun all the way around, trying to hit the thing. No one laughed.

The next pitch was the last chance he was gonna get. I came up behind Jake, closer to him than I'd been on the trolley on the way to the game earlier that day. I put my hands over his hands, made his knees bend slightly by nudging my knees into the back of his legs.

And Frank sent the ball right to us. We swung. The ball smacked against the broomstick.

Jake stood at home plate, stunned.

"I hit the ball, Joe. I hit it!"

Frank could easily have stooped down and scooped the ball up on its way past.

He let it go. Let it roll to outfield.

"Run, Jake," I yelled. "Run to first base!"

Jake started shuffling, still carrying the broomstick.

"Drop the bat," I yelled.

Jake dropped the stick midway to first base as Ira crossed home.

Lenny picked the ball up. But instead of throwing it to first base and knocking Jake out, he threw it to center field.

As Al crossed home plate we all yelled at Jake to run, run!

Center field threw the ball to second even though Jake had already left on his way to third.

Gus crossed home plate next, bringing the score from 6–0 to 6–3.

Second threw the ball to third just as Jake left on the last leg of the sweetest trip he'd ever taken in his entire life.

And then Jake, crazy arms, crazy legs Jake came flying over home plate!

Everybody, up and down Hancock Street, everybody went wild. Jumping up and down, yelling and screaming. Like we'd been the Superbas taking the pennant.

Jake. Ah, man, Jake. His face. You shoulda seen him. Jake was a hero. Better than Dirty Jack Doyle on his best day. A hundred times better than Dirty Jack.

What we'd been playing, it was nothing but a kid's game. With a broomstick for a bat. And a homemade ball.

But tonight, it was the American dream.

And we'd all gotten lucky.

MATTIE SCHMIDT

To see them on the street during the day they looked shabby and ill kept, lost to the world. When Mattie Schmidt arrived under the bridge, he'd already had a head start on madness. His mother had perished on a voyage from Europe. Mattie's father had locked himself and Mattie inside their house. He told Mattie someone wanted to kill them so they wouldn't ask questions about the death of Mattie's mother.

Where is her body? *his father kept saying.* They can't tell me where her body went.

Mattie's house began to change into a wild place, an abandoned place where only rats and roaches and feral cats lived. But Mattie and his father lived there, too, getting hungry and hungrier, crazy and crazier.

Finally the neighbors complained. They said they were worried about little Mattie. When the police came, they put Mattie's father in jail. They tried putting Mattie somewhere, too. But it was too late for Mattie, who was already crazy from eating things no one should eat. It was easy for Mattie to elude the police. He'd learned how to disappear right in front of his father's eyes. It had made the old man crazier and that made Mattie feel more alive.

So Mattie gave the police the slip and ran and ran and ran until he came to the bridge. And then he ducked under it and found the children. Oh, he liked the tough boys the best, and stood before them with his hands on his hips, his hair wild, a thick brown thatch.

I'm staying here, *he said.* With you.

The tough boys circled him. Max and Karl, Dickie and Otto, they circled him and told him to turn around so they could see him from all sides. Mattie turned, cocking his head defiantly. He had no fear. When your mother has died at sea and your father has gone crazy, locking you in the house, leaving you to figure how to stay alive, and you do stay alive, what is there to fear from a gang of tough boys? So he turned, and turned, slowly, and Dickie said,

Why not?

Because Dickie knew a brother when he saw one. They shook hands, Dickie and Mattie, Dickie who never touched anyone, not even The Bride. He took Mattie's hand and shook it and the two grinned their rabid grins at each other, knowing they could either love each other or kill each other, even if Mattie was only half Dickie's size. Mattie had a crazy meanness about him that Dickie knew well.

Dickie and Mattie, they chose to be on the same side. It made sense, even though they lived under a bridge and were too crazy to know if anything made sense.

The red roofs and quaint gray gables against the blue sky, the glitter of the lagoon, the rush and splash of the chutes . . . the stately elephant moving through the crowd . . . all these go with the price of admission to the grounds, and are the biggest dime's worth to be had at Coney or anywhere else.

—THE BROOKLYN DAILY EAGLE

CHAPTER FIFTEEN

WITH THE CANDY STORE CLOSED, Papa used the entire shop now for bear business. The glass window no longer drew customers. Papa didn't have time for window dressing. We made bears, only bears, and we sold them as fast as we made them.

Every morning, the outside lady stitchers went home with bear pieces. When they returned, they delivered batches of finished bears. Emily and I helped sort and pack, carefully matching each contract with the correct number of bears. Sometimes I helped with the cutting, too, when we had too many orders we couldn't keep up. Mama, with her beautiful penmanship, did all of the addressing. A wagon picked the bears up from our Tompkins Avenue doorstep regularly. Every day Mr. Kromer serenaded the parade of bears moving in and out of 404 Tompkins Avenue.

The inside ladies came every morning, too, but they sat at their tables and made bears under Papa's direction. Mama continued to go out with Lizzie regularly, looking for a place to move the ever-expanding bear business.

Emily asked one night at dinner, all of us gathered around the table, if she could use the front window for her own business. "You don't use it anymore, Papa."

"What business, Emily?" Mama asked, passing the green beans to Papa.

"The city approved our family for a home library," Emily said, just barely containing her excitement.

Emily had been talking to me about this home library for two months now. I couldn't believe it was really going to happen.

"The entire city of New York approved us?" Mama asked.

"I read about this in the paper," Uncle Meyer said.

"Yes, I did, too," said Lizzie Kaplan.

"What's a home library?" Papa asked.

Uncle Meyer explained. "Small collections of books are placed in private homes. Maybe the library is preparing to build a branch in a neighborhood and they want to test the water. Schoolchildren run these home operations out of their rooms, their kitchens, their . . ."

"Their front windows," Emily said. "The books are delivered here. Then, anyone in the neighborhood who wants to borrow comes to us."

"And you're proposing, Emily, to make our overcrowded store into a library?" Mama asked.

"She's proposing she set up the library in the store window," I said. "She's right. We're not using it anymore."

"You want people to climb up into the window to get something to read?" Papa asked.

Emily leaned forward. "They'll like that part. They'll like being in the window."

"Do you get money for this?" Papa asked.

"No, Papa."

"It's public service," Lizzie said.

When Emily first started talking about a home library, it took me a while to warm to the idea. It would be just one more thing to separate us from our neighbors. To call attention to us. Make us look better than the rest. But after a while I started to hope, with a library in our store window, maybe we'd be important to the neighborhood again in a good way, the way we were when we were a candy store.

"My Emily," Mama said, smiling. "A public servant. A librarian. I like this idea."

Papa shook his head no. "I need the front window. I'm sorry, *mamaleh*. Until we find a bigger place to run the bear business I need every square inch."

I cast a sympathetic glance at my sister. Her dark head lowered, she stared at her empty plate.

Mama knew what Emily wanted. "Morris," Mama said. "May I have a moment alone with you?"

WHILE EMILY prepared our shop window, Ida Winford, librarian, picked the books she thought might do well at 404 Tompkins Avenue. Emily never met Ida L. Winford. She had only letters from her. Emily imagined Miss Winford standing inside a cavern of books, rows and rows of books to every side of her, selecting the titles she thought kids in Brooklyn wanted to read. Ida Winford maybe knew books. I hoped she knew Brooklyn.

"Oh, she does, Joe. Librarians know everything."

I laughed. "Emily, you think she says to herself, 'Hmm, let me see. I have a million books here. Which ones should I send to Emily Michtom?'"

"Yeah," Emily said. "That's exactly what she thinks. What else?"

"Maybe she'll give us what nobody else wants. We get the duds."

"Why would she do that, Joe? It doesn't make sense."

"Of course it does. It gets all the bad books that never get read off her shelves."

"But Joe, if she sends bad books, then nobody takes them off our shelves, either, and we're a failure and she went to all that trouble approving us and sending us stuff for nothing. I think she sends books Tompkins Avenue will love. I think she picks the most popular books she knows and buys extra copies for libraries like ours."

"And what does she do with her duds, Emily?"

"Maybe she's so smart, Ida L. Winford, maybe she doesn't have duds."

"How about *Little Brother and Sister*?"

"Okay, so maybe we'll get some duds, but somebody might like *Little Brother and Sister*, even if we didn't."

I WASHED the plate glass, inside and out. Mr. Kromer lowered his clarinet and complimented us on our labor. Dilly stopped outside with his cart and grinned through the glass.

Emily scrubbed the floor inside the window with a rag, her arm dipping in and out of the pail. Benjamin grunted and hoisted himself inside the window to be with us every chance he got, dragging his bear along with him. He kept putting his grimy little hand all over the clean window.

"Benjamin, do not touch the glass!"

Several voices called from inside the shop, "Joseph, do not yell at the baby!"

I could see Emily's home branch of the public library was going to be more public than even she'd bargained for.

Emily and I tried to move the old drop-leaf table into the window, but no matter how many times I let her rest, she just couldn't lift it high enough and I couldn't get it all by myself.

Papa, who was still a little uncertain about losing his storefront, did not offer to help.

In the end, Uncle Meyer lifted the furniture into the window with me. In addition to the table we managed to come up with one high-backed chair and a glass-front bookcase. All of this furniture compliments of Mama, who liked taking breaks outside so she could admire our progress.

"Do you think I'll need more shelves for books?" Emily asked.

"If Miss Winford sends too many books," I said, "you can save some of the extras and put out fresh choices every few days."

"Like Papa used to do with the candy."

"Yeah. Exactly. It keeps the customer interested. Keeps 'em coming back."

Emily's library started attracting a crowd as soon as we moved the furniture into the window. The table and chair and bookcase sat empty, waiting, and kids stopped by two, three times a day, asking when the books would come. I was starting to love the little window of furniture almost as much as I loved the candy displays. Not a stuffed bear in sight. And kids coming to us all friendly.

And then, one day the wagon arrived, delivering Emily's books.

Just before opening the first box, Emily looked up at me, worried. "Do you really think they're all duds, Joe?"

I could hear how nervous she was, Emily, calm, fly-on-the-wall, know-it-all, nose-in-a-book Emily. I laughed. "Only one way to find out."

Emily had nothing to worry about. Miss Winford had come through for Brooklyn in a big way. If these books were duds, then they were just the kind of duds kids in Brooklyn would eat up.

"*Black Beauty*," Emily said with awe, pulling out the first title.

I reached inside the box next and came out with *Evangeline*. I didn't feel too excited about reading either *Black Beauty* or *Evangeline*, but whatever a fourteen-year-old straight-up Brooklyn guy might say about them, they were definitely not duds. It looked like we wouldn't be visiting the library at Avon Hall on the corner of Bedford and Halsey anytime soon. For the first time I could remember, Emily had more books than she could possibly read.

And the pile kept growing.

"*Aladdin and His Wonderful Lamp. Little Lord Fauntleroy. Jack and the Beanstalk. Sinbad the Sailor.*" When Emily recited the titles, they sounded like ice-cream orders at the soda fountain.

Not a hint of disappointment entered Emily's voice. She was wonder struck by this delivery of the wisdom of the world to our doorstep, in awe of the fact that suddenly she was the keeper of the words.

I put my hands on Wilson's *History Reader* and opened the book to the table of contents. Slowly I moved through the pages.

Looking up, I saw for the first time the crowd of kids. They watched us, salivating. Like we still had candy in the window. I remember once thinking the window was like an open book. And now it really was an open book.

There were practical books, too. In with the French novels there were books on mechanics, electricity, history, sociology. And books on music and art.

I handed Emily each book carefully and she arranged it on the bookcase, supporting it until she placed the next one beside it. Mama and Papa and all the sewing ladies had joined the crowd outside, watching Emily's home library being born.

We were nearly completely unpacked when Papa appeared. "Here, *mamaleh*," he said.

He had taken one of our best bowls from the kitchen and filled it with peppermint candies. "So each of your customers will taste the sweetness that comes with knowledge," Papa said. "So that my daughter will taste the sweetness of a successful business."

I didn't want to tell him you shouldn't read and eat at the same time. I know Emily did it whenever she could get away with it. But I hoped Miss Winford, librarian, would forgive my sister if some of the books happened to get a little bit sticky.

Emily placed the bowl on the upper-right corner of the table. She sat down in the librarian's chair as I went through the shop, out the door, and instructed the customers to please stand for a line. One at a time I ushered Emily's library patrons in through the shop, into the window, where Emily invited them to take their time browsing.

Even after we went upstairs for dinner that night, people came, not just kids, but grown-ups, calling up to us from the street, their voices floating through the kitchen window, asking if Emily could come down and open the library just for a minute.

My sister was in business.

THE BOY WITH THE VIOLIN

No one could say why the police didn't round them up, the children under the bridge, why the police didn't carry them off to the station, put them in prisons, orphanages, asylums. But they never patrolled under that part of the bridge, not at night.

Daylight brought footsteps and curious eyes. People walked there, or rode past. But the place was so dark, so grim, so rank, so filled with the broken and unwanted that people went right past without looking too close. It had become a place of garbage, and wounded animals, and bad dreams. The children arranged it to appear that way. They abandoned it during the hours when someone might be looking, even for them. They came back to reclaim it only after nightfall.

In their short lives, if they'd ever gone to school, or the theater, or sat in a restaurant and had food brought to them, that was their old world. Their life before the bridge.

But one night a boy arrived under the bridge and from the first sight of him the others knew he was different.

This new boy's fingers were long, clean, elegant. He wore a fine suit and hat, a tie and a gleaming white shirt. His face was scrubbed, fed, soft.

But his eyes held secrets. He arrived with a black leather valise in one hand, a violin case in the other, and neither of these would he let go. He kept one hand always on that violin case as jealously as Dickie kept his eyes on The Bride. The boy with the violin seemed frightened at first, particularly of the tough boys like Dickie, whose bruises had faded, but whose broken face had healed wrong.

The boy with the violin first appeared in the middle of the night. He'd have liked to come to rest near The Bride, but Dickie's head lifted and growled, and so the boy approached instead Helen and Nina.

The girls woke when the boy neared their sleepy nest of newspapers and moth-eaten blankets. They began to protest but the boy sat down anyway. He placed the violin case on his lap. Lovingly, he opened the lid and, lifting the instrument out, nestled it under his jaw. He began to play, softly. So softly. Afraid the sound would travel and give him away, but still needing to play, needing, needing to play.

The bow moved like a butterfly, up and down, over and back. It was the only way the boy knew to speak to them, explain to them that he had a right to be there, too.

The violin told a long story and the children sighed to hear it. Willie, who would sometimes pace at night like a caged wolf, settled down, unknotted his scarf, stroked his face with the filthy cloth, remembering his mother.

Those who woke stared into the darkness under the bridge and saw something beautiful there, over their heads, something born out of the notes the boy with the violin played. And the ones who slept, well, they dreamed. Such dreams. Such rich dreams. Dreams that lingered into the next day, filling them with a sense of the majesty to be found even under a bridge with the dirty East River rolling past.

The boy with the violin made his quiet confession to the children. The music told that the boy was a thief. That he had stolen this violin, this instrument made by the son of Stradivarius, worth more than a long block of tenement houses. The violin meant so much to the boy that he would rather be lost to the world than surrender it to its legal owner. The song told the children how the violin could come alive only if the boy played it. It had chosen him as much as he had chosen it. And the children knew that if they took that violin from him and tried to sell it, the children knew the violin would turn to dust in their hands.

And besides, if they left the boy and the violin alone, if they made him feel at home under the bridge, he would stay. And play for them. And they would have music there, such music they'd never dreamed of. And so Helen and Nina crept off their nest of rags, and plumped it up, and patted it as if preparing the finest feather mattress. Helen, her mouth so wide it stretched nearly across her entire face, ending on either side in dimples, and Nina, whose ragged dress came down long enough to cover her scabbed legs, the two surrendered their space.

And the boy nodded, placed the violin lovingly back in its case, curled around his instrument, and motioned for the girls to return so he might share their warmth, so he might sleep without the guilt of having stolen something as important as someone's bed, so the music inside him could spill over a little and sweeten their dreams, too.

However one approaches Coney Island, whether by boat or train, one lands near the heart of things. And Luna Park has made good claim as the "heart of Coney Island."

—THE BROOKLYN DAILY EAGLE

CHAPTER SIXTEEN

EVER SINCE LUNA PARK OPENED at Coney Island, I'd had my hopes pinned on getting there.

Lenny and Gus, Al and Mike and Mitch had already gone with their families.

But not the Michtoms. Even with Pauline's Russian making things easier, even with all Uncle Meyer did, Mama and Papa couldn't take time for a night out. Forget about spending a whole day at Coney.

And so they worked. Night and day. I don't think they'd taken a break once since Papa set the first two bears in the shop window, except to bury The Queen.

Sorting bears day after day, I realized that if I wanted to go to Coney, I'd have to get there on my own.

Unfortunately, you couldn't just go to Coney Island. You needed carfare. You needed money at the gate. And then you needed extra for the rides.

The rides were the best, that's what the guys said. Al said, "Even the trip down Ocean Parkway, just getting there, is something." Frank said, "Don't tell him anything. You'll ruin it." Mitch, who made fun of everything, he didn't make fun of Coney.

A lot of kids my age worked outside their homes for wages, but my parents wouldn't allow that. They kept me busy. Emily, too, who now split her summer between taking care of Benjamin and taking care of the library. Neither of us got a dime for our efforts. If I was going to Coney, that had to change.

"I need some spending money," I told Mama, gazing at her over a nearly full box of bears.

"You need what?"

"I'm working every day for you and Papa. I could be out working for someone else, earning money. You and Papa don't give me anything."

"We don't give you anything?" Papa said.

"We should give you money? To live under our roof? To eat our food? To be our son?" Mama asked. "You don't want to belong to this family anymore, Joseph?"

"You're getting it all wrong, Mama. I just want to have a little money in my pocket."

Papa chimed in. "You and the rest of the world. Listen to me, Joseph Michtom. You don't know how lucky you got it. You have a lifetime to put money in your pocket. There's plenty time for a real job. You only get to be a boy once. So be a boy. Some people, they don't even get that."

Mama continued the lecture. "What's the matter? You

don't get enough to eat here? You don't have a place to sleep? Go out, Mr. Empty Pockets. Go out and look around Brooklyn. Go across the bridge and walk around the Lower East Side and then come back and tell me you're suffering. You convince me you have it bad and we'll talk. Until then, end of story."

Papa and Mama had spoken.

I had no one to intercede for me the way Mama interceded with Papa for the rest of the world. Certainly not Uncle Meyer. He always took Mama's side. Not Lizzie Kaplan, either. She'd never contradict Mama or Papa when it came to how they raised their children.

Coney Island, it became clear to me, that would be a place everyone else went.

Emily carried Benjamin on her hip into the shop window. They started shelving books.

"Joseph," Mama called. "You've been standing over that box ten minutes. What's the matter with you?"

"Nothing," I scowled.

Benjamin wiggled out of Emily's arms, slid down from the shop window, and rushed toward me, lifting his bear to my face.

"Pay wif me, Osif. Pay wif me."

Benjamin danced the bear up and down my legs.

I growled at my brother and his stupid bear. Not a play growl, either. A real one.

Benny's eyes widened. He pulled his bear close to his chest, burst into tears, and ran back to Emily.

Mama raised an eyebrow and frowned at me.

But Papa had had enough. "Out," he said. "Out, Joseph. And don't show your face until you can be a civil member of this family."

AND OUT I went. What? This was punishment? That I should be liberated from the chains of the shop? That I be sent outside on a summer afternoon? That I have time to myself? This kind of punishment was going to hurt me?

The sound of Mr. Kromer's clarinet faded as I stormed toward Fulton Street. I crossed and kept going, beyond Atlantic, toward Prospect Park. I kept my eyes down. Sometimes you find something on the ground. Sometimes a penny, a nickel, maybe even a quarter. Me? Lucky Joe Michtom? I found nothing.

But I kept walking. Trying to burn off the anger.

Don't come back until I can be a civil member of the family? Fine. Fine! I'd never come back. How would they like that?

I had planned to search for Uncle Meyer's waterfall once I got to the park but I changed my mind. I didn't want the waterfall. I didn't want to be soothed. I liked feeling the anger. It made me feel grown up.

I kept walking down the green paths of the park, from the north end to the south, and then out and onto Ocean Parkway. Al had said how great Ocean Parkway was. He was right. It was beautiful. Wide and clean.

As I walked, the afternoon wound down and slowly turned into evening. My anger was winding down, too, but I kept going. One foot in front of the other. It felt good just to be moving, and

I knew now where I was going. I'd been heading there all along.

To Coney Island.

All the way to Coney.

On my own two feet.

People on bicycles sped past in both directions. If I still had my wheel, it would have been easy to get to Coney. But ever since the time I fell in the street when I was nine, Mama and Papa refused to let me near another bicycle. So it would have to be on foot or not at all.

I DON'T KNOW when it hit me that I was really out of my neighborhood. Ever since I was little Mama forbade me to wander. I knew bad things could happen to you. Even with an adult around, I knew bad things could happen.

But I kept going anyway. I felt safe on the parkway. Everyone I passed nodded, tipped hats, smiled.

Maybe I couldn't get inside Luna Park, but I could at last stand there. That wouldn't cost anything.

And it would be Coney.

And I would be there.

That would be enough.

BY THE TIME I reached Coney Island I hurt everywhere. My feet burned, my legs screamed, my eyes blurred, my head throbbed, I was covered in sweat. I smelled Red Hots, popped corn, taffy. Hunger stung my stomach like a swarm of bees.

Though the sun had already set, the sky was bright over

Coney. A hat of light hovered in the air. The entrance to Luna Park, when I finally stood before it, nearly blinded me. Lit by thousands of lights. I saw now what the guys meant. It looked like the best dream you could ever have. Like fairyland and heaven all rolled into one. Only you didn't have to be asleep or dead to get in.

You just had to have a dime.

And I didn't have a dime.

People, so many people entering at the gate. They laughed, shouted, leaned into one another. In all of Coney Island, I was the only person hungry and alone.

I wished for my sister, Emily. Not Ira. Not Mitch. Not even Gus. I wished for Emily. I didn't know anyone who would love all this more. I wanted her to see it. She might even figure a way to get us in.

I couldn't risk trying to sneak in. That would kill Mama. If I should get arrested for entering Luna Park without a ticket.

I sat on the curb and rested awhile, haunted by the smell of food. There were things frying and baking and steaming no matter which direction I turned, and if I let myself think about it my mouth ran with juice. Just the way it did when I thought about Dilly's pickles.

Raw, oozing blisters crippled my feet. I needed to cool them. Limping away from the lights, I left the boardwalk and dropped onto the beach.

Before long I had my shoes and socks off. My heart beat hard in my chest. I hadn't been alone this close to the water since . . . since . . .

I felt terror and excitement all at once.

Under darkness, at the edge of the black sea, I yelped as the salt stung my open blisters. But eventually my feet sighed with relief despite the sting. I moved along the fringe of water, carrying my shoes and socks.

On an impulse, I stripped off all my clothes. Wearing only my cotton union suit, I waded into the black Atlantic. I told myself I'd be safe. I'd only go far enough to get wet. Not even up to my waist.

I'd never done anything like this before. It felt good. I felt free. Never, since I was a little boy, had I felt this free. The feeling lasted maybe an hour. No more. Because as the heat of the day, the heat of my anger with my parents, the heat of my frustration all melted away and drained out of my body, all I felt was exhaustion.

And that's the first time I considered how I would get back home. I had nothing left, no reserve energy to walk that long distance in reverse.

And even if I did, I wouldn't get home until the middle of the night, maybe not until morning.

My parents were going to kill me. The folly of Joseph Michtom, I thought, standing waist deep in the cool salt water. What you gonna do now, Joe? Big-shot grown-up Joseph Michtom, son of the famous maker of stuffed bears. You lucky guy, you. How you gonna fill your empty stomach? How you gonna get yourself back up Ocean Parkway through Brooklyn to 404 Tompkins Avenue?

Boats made from woven rattan start revolving close to the ground, gradually ascending to a height of sixty feet. At night, lighted by 2,000 incandescent lamps, they look like whirling rings of flame.

—THE NEW YORK TIMES

CHAPTER SEVENTEEN

I STAYED IN THE WATER a long time. Long enough I started shivering. When I splashed back out, I found the place where I'd left my clothes. But my clothes weren't there.

My clothes weren't there!

I made ever-widening circles, searching for my blue shirt, my pincheck pants, my shoes, my socks, my gray cap. I scoured the beach, going over the same places, again and again. Surely I'd missed them. The next time I checked I would find my little pile of clothes, they'd be right where I'd left them.

But they weren't. They were gone.

Finally I had to admit to myself that someone had come along while I was in the water and taken my clothes, leaving me only my sagging, wet underwear, cold and clammy, clinging to my skin.

THE ABSENCE OF MAY

The next time the Radiant Boy came he ignored the parrot, and Willie, and Helen and Nina, and he glided up to May. He stared at her. He did not slide his finger across his throat. He did not touch her. He just stared at her. He came night after night. Each time he'd come only for May, staring at her, until he glided off.

After five nights, when May woke, again, to the torment of the Radiant Boy, she crept out from under the bridge, crept out of his reach, and fled, covering her mouth, which had finally started to heal. She ran away from the bridge, away from the Radiant Boy, away from the safety and comfort of the other children, because no one could save her from a ghost. And fleeing through the night streets of Brooklyn, down Furman to Pineapple, down Hicks to Pierrepont, her breath burning in her throat, her chest exploding with pain, she ran directly into the large, uniformed officer on patrol.

Easy there, girlie, *the officer said, catching May and holding her firmly.* Where are you off to in such a hurry?

And just like that she collapsed in his arms because suddenly there was a pain inside May so great she knew it would kill her. And if the officer had not carried her to the hospital right then, the surgeons said it would have been too late. Instead, doctors worked through the night, operating on May, repairing some little bit of damage left over from her meal of carbolic acid, a little bit of hurt that had managed to turn into something festered and septic and deadly inside her.

And having survived her surgery, off she was taken when she could be safely moved, a vagrant, consigned to the House of the Good Shepherd, where the girls on her floor tried to befriend her. And they nearly did. Three girls, Della, Vinnie, and Till. They got her to talking, finally talking—imagine, May talking—and though she wouldn't talk about what had happened to her before the acid, she did tell about her life under the bridge. About the parrot and Karl and Max and The Bride. And she said how the Radiant Boy saved her life because if he hadn't chased her from under the bridge, she would have died there in the night. But instead she ran into the policeman and he carried her to the hospital and the surgeons repaired her stomach and that's why she was alive. And that made twice that she almost died, once because she drank acid and again because she drank acid, though she didn't mean for the second time. That part of her life was over. That cutting, acid-taking part. It really was.

Her three new friends, Della, Vinnie, and Till, they wanted to see with their own eyes. They wanted to hear the naughty parrot, and see Dickie and The Bride, and sleep under the bridge. So one night, when the four fourth-floor girls were certain the Sisters had retired, they unmade their beds and tied their sheets together. *And the pillow-cases, too. And May tied their rope of sheets to her bed, throwing the tail of the linens out the window.*

I'll go first, *she said.*

No wait, *Della said.* How do we know you won't just run off as soon as you get to the bottom?

And May could tell they didn't trust her, that they'd never trusted her, and they didn't believe her about the bridge and the parrot and maybe they weren't her friends after all because no one ever really was.

And she said, gruffly, I won't run off.

But Vinnie said, No, we'll go first.

And so little Till climbed over the windowsill, and hand over hand, lowered herself until she reached the end of the bed linen rope. But there was a gap, twenty feet at least, between Till and the ground. And not knowing whether to go back up or drop, she hung on a few seconds more and let go.

May heard Till's leg break four flights up, and without any thought to her own safety she hurried out the window, down the rope, and dropped, dropped, dropped through the summer air, landing, unhurt, on the ground beside Till.

Till's eyes went wide with wonder because May hadn't fallen. May had flown down those last twenty feet like a great white bird. And while Till pondered the mystery of May's flight, May ran to the Sister on call and brought her to Till, who was treated with the greatest care, because it was, after all, a very nice place, the House of the Good Shepherd, and while Till was being fussed over, May slipped away, suddenly free of the Sisters and their locked doors.

She eluded the night dangers, hiding in shadows, behind ash cans, pressing herself against brick walls. And at last she made her way back under the bridge before dawn, where the children woke to find her.

Nina and Helen said, Come sit with us.

Imagine that.

May sat her bony rump down at the foot of the nest where Nina and Helen and the boy with the violin slept and said,

Thank you,

and the sun rose, evicting the sharp-shouldered children from under the bridge for one more day.

From first to last the audience feels the thrill of danger. It does not realize how great the danger, but there is no clowning with lions and tigers and jaguars.

—THE BROOKLYN DAILY EAGLE

CHAPTER EIGHTEEN

I DON'T KNOW HOW LONG I SAT on the beach, looking back toward Coney's lights, wondering what to do.

Strangers had come.

They had taken my clothes.

But I was alive.

I was still alive.

Nothing *bad* had happened to me. Nothing. Really. Bad. I'd gone into the water and come out again and all that I'd lost were my clothes.

After maybe an hour, a man wandered over and sat on the beach beside me. He had a gray goatee. He wore a paint-stained beret.

"Good swim?" he asked.

I wrapped my arms around myself, trying to keep my teeth from chattering. "Yeah," I answered. "Best swim I had my entire life."

The man nodded.

"Someone take your clothes?" he asked.

I stared out into the black Atlantic.

"Looks like it."

"Damn street kids . . ."

"Do you know who did it?"

"It's always the street kids. Who else?" he said.

I had no fear of this man. All my life I'd been wary of strangers, uneasy with leaving home, terrified of water. Now, here I was, alone with a stranger, miles from home, at the ocean. And I wasn't afraid. At least not of him.

"This is a good spot," he said. "This is my favorite place to come. I can think here. A man needs a place to think sometimes, you know?"

I nodded.

"Police got a station not far from here. Why don't you go report the theft?"

"Can't," I said.

"You in trouble?"

"No. I'm in my underwear."

"So drop in at the charity tent beside the station and get yourself some clothes."

"Can't," I said.

"Why not?"

"I'm in my underwear."

"You want to come home with me? Maybe you'll fit into something of mine. It's okay. I used to have a son."

This guy was crazy.

I thanked him for his offer but told him I didn't think I could come home with him just now.

"Suit yourself," the man said. Then he laughed at his own joke. A dry, sad sort of laugh. He stood, brushed sand off himself, and walked away.

"Suit yourself," he repeated, muttering, as darkness closed around him.

He might have brought back some clothes for me to put on. Papa would have done as much. Uncle Meyer, too. But not every man was a Morris Michtom or a Meyer Marshak. Bringing clothes to me never occurred to this man. He simply got up and walked away.

Maybe he thought it was my problem. I had to solve it.

Maybe he was right.

LUNA PARK had closed. Most of Coney Island had closed. Occasionally someone crossed Surf Avenue on foot. Mostly, though, everyone had gone home, climbed their own stairs, gotten between their sheets. They'd gone back to where they belonged. Closed their eyes, let go of the day, the good of it, the bad of it. They were home, and that was everything.

New York law prohibited walking in the street in swimming clothes. How much worse, I thought, to parade up Surf Avenue in my underwear. And so I sat on the beach, shivering.

But after I'd gone numb, head to toe, I knew I couldn't sit

any longer. Standing, I brushed dried sand from my skin, waiting for the prickling to stop in my feet.

POLICE HEADQUARTERS stood out from the other buildings at the business end of Coney Island. Easy to find. The charity tent across from it, too. The only two places on Coney still showing any sign of life. But I couldn't bring myself to enter either place. The charity tent was full of strangers. What would they do to me? What would they say? I didn't feel like a big man anymore. I was just a stupid kid who ran away from home and couldn't even hold on to his own clothes.

After hiding outside the charity tent for a while, trying to work up the courage to go in, I saw a man limp out in my direction. Drawing into the shadows, I hoped he wouldn't notice me. He hobbled right past. But a moment later he turned, came back to my hiding place, which must have been no hiding place at all. The man looked me over. Without a word he reentered the relief tent, moving so smoothly on his gimpy leg I thought he must have been lame his whole life. The man reemerged from the tent with a mug of hot coffee. He put the mug in my hands. Nodded. Then limped away.

Shivering, I took a sip of the coffee. The man had loaded it with milk and sugar. More milk and sugar, in fact, than actual coffee. I wished I could wrap my whole body around that mug. The warmth of it made a trail down my throat to my stomach. It felt like anyone looking at me could see the journey that coffee was taking.

Somewhere in the distance church bells struck 3 A.M. I still couldn't bring myself to enter the charity tent or the police station and started moving away, staying, whenever possible, in the shadows.

Suddenly an automobile came tearing down the street. At just the same moment a little dog was crossing. It was nothing but a mutt. A little brown mutt making its way from one side of Surf Avenue to the other. And then the mutt and the automobile, they were in the same place, at the same time. And then the automobile sped away and the dog lay in the road. It was so quiet on Coney Island that all I could hear was that soft thump, over and over again in my ears.

I emerged from the shadows and walked to the edge of the street near the dog. It lifted its head and whined. I don't know about dogs, hurt or not. But I sat down on the curb and started talking to it. I thought about The Queen in her white sheets and told the dog not to be afraid.

"It hasn't been such a great night for me, either," I said and started telling the dog all about my day. The dog pulled itself up, limped closer to me, put its head under my hand. I stroked the dog's head and kept talking.

After an hour or so the dog stood and without giving me another look, shook itself gently, whined, licked gingerly at a spot on its side, and limped away.

* * *

THE SKY was starting to lighten. In my underwear, being on such a busy street as Surf Avenue seemed like a bad idea. So I headed back to the beach.

The sun rose slowly. Before it appeared it sent advance streamers across the sky. Silver. And purple. And pink. And then I saw the sun itself, a ball of fire. It was burning, like my stomach, wavering as it lifted itself out of the ocean.

People started returning, arriving at the beach for a day of pleasure. And here I was, still in my underwear.

Most people didn't even notice me. They moved past me, absorbed in their own worlds. I was just a boy, sitting in the sand, hoping the sun would warm me, my skin blue and pop-pled with gooseflesh.

And then a little girl, about the same age as Benjamin, ran over to me. She gripped a stuffed bear in her hand and seeing her, seeing that bear, I knew I'd lost everything. That I could never go back. My luck had finally run out. At Coney Island.

The little girl's mother rushed over and grabbed her. She looked at me, first suspicious, then confused, then curious.

"You okay, kid?" she asked.

I shook my head no.

I told her someone had stolen my clothes and I'd been out all night.

"Go home," she said.

I told her I was a long way from home. That I lived north

of Fulton Street. I'd walked, I said. I didn't know how I was gonna get back.

"From north of Fulton?" She shook her head in wonder. "Your mother must be worried sick about you."

I nodded.

"Go to the charity tent and tell them you need clothes. You hear me? Then tell them you need a way home. You walked all the way here from north of Fulton?"

I nodded, not trusting myself to talk.

Her little daughter pulled at her now, eager to move on.

"You hear me?" she said, as they stepped away. "Go to the charity tent."

And so I returned to the tent and this time I went inside and told them everything, even the part about having a fight with my parents. It was so easy. I don't know why I couldn't do it before.

The ladies in the tent fixed me up with some clothes, a cup of coffee, a roll; they escorted me across to police headquarters.

The police got me home by lunchtime.

GUY

Where the children went during the day was mostly their own business. There were times when they passed one another. They didn't stop, or speak. They acknowledged one another, but a stranger might not notice the gesture at all.

Daily, Guy traveled farther from the bridge than any of the others. Occasionally he saw Mattie or Max and Karl, even Otto and Willie from time to time, but he never passed Dickie. He knew he wouldn't. That's because Dickie wouldn't be caught dead in the neighborhood Guy loved most. Prospect Park. Where Dickie's father had pounded Dickie within an inch of his life.

Guy would look at the grand houses and wonder which was Dickie's, which of the men he saw carrying out garbage, or holding the door to a carriage, or polishing an automobile, which of those would be Dickie's father, a man who would beat his own flesh and blood to death?

But that's not what brought Guy to Prospect Park day after day, week after week. It was the sheep. And their shepherd. The flock belonged to the Prospect Park menagerie. And somehow Guy felt he belonged to the flock.

Guy remembered his homeland only barely. He remembered a room with a stove, and the boat that brought them to the crowded tenement basement, on the crowded block, where no one searched very hard when someone went missing because there were already so many, so, so many mouths to feed.

But the shepherd of Prospect Park, Mr. O'Hara, made Guy feel safe and happy, and so the boy made the long walk from the bridge each morning, and the long walk back each afternoon, spending the day on the grass, watching Mr. O'Hara and his two dogs, Laddie and Topsy, and their great flock of sheep, more than a hundred, grazing in Prospect Park. And Guy thought it would be good to have such a job. Two dogs who watched his every move, who hung on his every whistle and word, and a fleecy mass of sheep to watch over and tend.

Mr. O'Hara noticed the boy. How could he help but notice him? He noticed the boy with his red hair and his dark cap and his bare feet. But although the boy kept his eyes on the shepherd as faithfully as the dogs did, he didn't come to the shepherd when called, he didn't look to him for commands. He only watched.

And at the end of each day, when Mr. O'Hara and Laddie and Topsy led the sheep back to their shelter, the barefooted boy set off, north by northwest, and the sun set him aglow so that James O'Hara didn't know for certain if the boy was real or some Irish spirit protecting them all from the devil.

CHAPTER NINETEEN

MAMA LOOKED UP WHEN I CAME IN through the shop door. Her eyes were nearly swollen shut from crying. It hurt to look at her.

Her expression went from relief to fury, then back to relief. Then back to fury.

"Papa's been out all night looking for you. How could you do this to us?"

"I'm sorry, Mama," I said. "I'm really sorry."

The policeman filled Mama in on how I spent the night.

"All the way to Coney Island he walked?" Mama said. "All the way to Coney Island?"

"That's some kid you got there, Mrs. Michtom. Any kid who can walk from here to Coney . . . well, that's some kid."

Mama didn't seem to hear anything the policeman was saying. She just kept shaking her head in disbelief. "All the way to Coney Island?"

Mama sent me upstairs to my room. Emily followed.

All I wanted was to get in bed and sleep. All Emily wanted was to talk.

She dug out her private candy stash and offered me her favorites.

Emily sat on the edge of my bed, studying my face with those serious eyes of hers.

Finally she said, "I missed you."

I remembered how much I'd wished for Emily to be with me when I first saw the lights of Coney Island.

"I missed you, too."

"Last night, when you were gone, Mama and Papa were so scared. They thought they'd never see you again. They cried. Papa, too, Joe. He cried. They thought I wasn't listening. I was listening, Joe. They talked and they cried. They kept saying it was 'like Stephen all over again. Just like Stephen.' Joe, who's Stephen?"

I knew who Stephen was. "He was somebody from long ago, Emily. You weren't even born."

"But who . . . ?"

"I'm tired, Em."

All these years I'd been waiting just to hear his name. All these years. And then last night, finally. Finally someone talked about Stephen. Because they were scared. Scared they'd lost me. Like Stephen was lost.

Emily sat quietly beside me.

How many times had I wanted to talk about Stephen, to

Mama and Papa, to Uncle Meyer, to The Queen. But I never knew how to start. And I was afraid. Afraid of how it would finish. Afraid that what happened to Stephen was my fault. My fault.

Now Emily waited.

She wanted me to talk about him.

And I couldn't.

THE BED felt so good. Our cramped room, it looked like heaven. I sighed. "I never thought I'd see this room again."

Emily looked around, trying to see the room the way I was seeing it.

She shrugged, tucked her hair behind her ears. "What was it like?" she asked.

"What was *what* like?"

"You know. Last night. Everything."

One of my blisters caught on the sheet and sent a shooting pain up and down my leg. I winced. "I figure it was probably the worst night of my life, Em." I put my arm under my head and shut my eyes. "But it was probably the best, too."

I thought Emily might understand what I meant. I thought I might understand better myself once I'd had some sleep and some time to think.

Emily touched my arm like I was a kind of hero. I could feel something coming off of her, like being fanned when it's really hot, only it wasn't a breeze coming from Emily, it was respect.

And I knew in that moment how it would feel to be Dirty Jack Doyle, star of the Superbas, with a starstruck kid looking into my face. Or even maybe the way it would feel to be President Theodore Roosevelt. The way Emily was treating me, that wasn't about being lucky. To Emily I wasn't just Lucky Joe. I was her big brother, the one who had walked all the way to Coney Island.

"Joe?"

I opened my eyes and gazed at Emily. "I'm pretty tired, Em."

She nodded. Stood. Went to the door.

But she didn't leave. I fell asleep with Emily watching over me.

THE SOUND OF BREAKING GLASS

The Radiant Boy came one night so late that most of the children had already found refuge in sleep. Dickie near The Bride, Max near Karl.

The boy with the violin played softly so close to deaf Frances she smiled in her sleep, feeling the vibrations.

Dickie and Mattie had spent the day collecting bottles. Each had managed to gather nearly a dozen to sell to the druggist. Mostly blue glass, some green. The druggist paid well for unchipped glass. The children would have food for days.

But the Radiant Boy glided in and where he went the sound of smashing glass followed.

Dickie and Mattie woke, and, quick to anger, believing their hard work and their promise of food had been destroyed by the boy in white, they yelled at him and chased after. And the boy with the violin put his instrument down and stared, his mouth wide open as the two hornet-wild boys crazily chased a ghost, a death-omen ghost.

The Radiant Boy paid no attention to Dickie or Mattie. It was the one with the violin he'd come after, stopping in front of him. The ghost looked at the boy with his round, soft cheeks. Peered at him. Lifted his hand to his throat. But May, May, oh, May, stepped between them, between the musician and the ghost. Lowering her head, she braced for the death sentence.

But the Radiant Boy's hand lowered again and he moved on, gliding smoothly, the glass still crashing as he passed, the sound of it echoing under the looming framework of the bridge. He left without rolling a finger across his neck. He left behind only the sound of smashing glass. It trailed after him.

When Dickie and Mattie checked the bottles they'd spent all day collecting, they found them unbroken, stacked inside the crates just as they'd left them. And Mattie scratched his head. And Dickie shrugged. And Helen stood and clapped her hands, smiling at May, brave May. And all the others joined in.

And the boy with the violin knelt before her and played just for May, played until everyone settled down and closed their eyes where the afterlight from the Radiant Boy lingered, though the memory of the smashing glass had already begun to fade.

The new superstructure, which begins close to the main entrance and surrounds the lagoon, is a promenade on stilts for the public, lined with Japanese tea gardens and banks of flowers. It is high enough to afford a view of everything going on in the grounds.

—THE NEW YORK TIMES

CHAPTER TWENTY

LIZZIE KAPLAN FOUND THE PERFECT PROPERTY for the bear business. We kept our flat and the shop on Tompkins Avenue, at least for the time being. But most of the business operations shifted to a loft on Fulton not far from Uncle Meyer's. Papa hired Mr. Rostowsky to paint a new sign.

Mr. Kromer put away his clarinet for a couple of days and helped with the move. It sure was quiet on the corner of Hancock and Tompkins without Mr. Kromer playing that horn.

After the move Mama said, "Joseph and Emily, I need you should look after Benjamin every day now. Yes?"

"What about when school starts, Mama? Are we supposed to skip school and look after him then, too?"

"Don't start, Joseph Michtom."

I had to be careful how I pushed my luck these days. Mama still hadn't forgiven me for running away and frightening her nearly to death.

"I'm advertising in the classifieds," Mama said. "We'll find a girl."

UNCLE MEYER and Lizzie continued to join us for dinner and sometimes Pauline Unger's Russian came, too. Occasionally Pauline herself put in an appearance, though she rarely spoke. Pauline had changed a lot since she'd gotten married.

It was funny. Pauline and Lizzie had started out as opposites. Pauline so outgoing. Lizzie so reserved. They were still opposites. But now they'd switched sides. The Queen had been right. It was better just to stay clear of women. All of them. I'd never understand them.

Mama and Papa, since my night on Coney Island, they treated me differently.

Not so much like a kid anymore.

For so long I'd wanted them to let me grow up. But I'd been afraid of it, too.

Now that it was happening, it wasn't so scary after all.

AT DINNER, and late into the night, our flat filled with talk, laughter, debate. When the business moved out, so did the constant reminders of bears. Some nights we'd have a letter from Aunt Lena, telling us about her travels. She'd rescued an orphan, Mary. Aunt Lena's letters described the little girl. Aunt Lena wrote asking Papa and Mama how they'd feel about having an adopted niece.

Emily had been thrilled. "I've always wanted a cousin."

Aunt Lena was nearly fifty. I wondered what it would be like to have such an old mother. But maybe little Mary thought having an old mother was better than having no mother at all. Especially if the mother was someone as kind as Aunt Lena.

Some nights Lizzie would entertain us with stories of Aunt Zelda and her gift for real estate. Aunt Zelda had bought and sold two properties already, making a nice profit each time. Lizzie said Aunt Zelda was gaining a reputation as an up-and-comer on the New York real-estate scene.

Some nights Papa and Lizzie told stories about Aunt Golda. I liked hearing about The Queen. I missed her.

Summer was nearly over and I'd hardly done anything. I'd walked to Coney Island, but I never got in.

I'd been to a game at Washington Park, but only one.

What kind of summer was that?

Emily at least had her library.

MAMA MEANT IT about me and Emily looking after Benjamin.

Every day, my brother stuck to me like chewing gum to a hot shoe.

One morning, before she left for Fulton Street, Mama packed a picnic.

"You kids take Benjamin to Prospect Park for the day. Here's a nickel for each of you. Go have fun."

"I have library hours today," Emily said.

"You'll put a sign in the window. You can have a vacation from the library. You think real librarians don't take vacations?"

We pushed Benny to Prospect Park in the wicker carriage seat. Sometimes he'd get out and hold my hand while Emily steered the empty chair. But after a while Benny's legs tired and he'd happily climb back in to be pushed again.

Wherever he went, his bear went with him.

I tried not to touch it. "Benny, that thing is disgusting."

Benjamin loyally wrapped his bear in his arms and turned his head away from me.

Emily frowned. "Hey, Joe. I can get Benjamin to the park myself if you want. You don't have to go."

"Mama would kill me."

"I wouldn't tell."

And I knew she wouldn't.

But Benjamin would.

"Thanks, Em," I said. "But we better not. Blabbermouth Michtom here would give us away."

"Where should we go then?"

I thought about the waterfall. I had promised myself I'd show them the waterfall after Benjamin recovered from pneumonia. Uncle Meyer had said he didn't mind if I shared his secret with my brother and sister.

But the spiteful side of me resisted.

"How about the menagerie?" Emily suggested.

I nodded.

All three of us liked visiting the animals.

WE CLIMBED past the sheep, up Sullivan Hill to the pens.

Emily liked the deer best.

Benjamin liked the seals and the stray cats.

And just to prove how contrary I'd become, I liked the bears. Go figure. With all the animals to choose from at Prospect Park, with the stuffed version of them the bane of my existence, I liked the bears.

Emily and I were sitting on a bench after lunch when a policeman strode over with a little girl in his arms. He sat down beside us.

The little girl clung to the policeman, but her eyes followed Benny and his bear as they played in the grass.

"That's a very loved bear," the policeman said.

Emily nodded. "It's the very first stuffed bear ever."

"Is it now?" said the policeman, humoring her.

Adults never believe kids.

The little girl in his arms didn't take her eyes off Benjamin's bear.

"Hey, Benny, you want to introduce your bear to the police officer?" I asked.

Benjamin came over.

"This is our brother, Benjamin," Emily said.

"Dis my bear."

The policeman extended his hand to Benjamin first, and then to the bear, shaking paws with both. "I'm Officer Henky," he said. "And this is Estelle."

Estelle looked straight at Benjamin and held both arms out. Even though she didn't do the gimme, gimme, it was clear what she wanted. She wanted Benny to hand over his bear. My brother was having none of it.

He ran away from the bench and started showing off, dancing crazy, stomping around, shouting nonsense words as he marched over the grass.

There was something about Estelle that made me want to go over and yank the bear away from Benjamin and hand it to her.

She wrapped her arms back around the beefy neck of Officer Henky and placed her head on his shoulder.

"Is she your daughter?" Emily asked.

"Orphan," Officer Henky said quietly. "I take her out every couple of weeks."

Emily told Officer Henky about Aunt Lena and the orphan she'd rescued.

"Benny," I called.

My brother came bouncing back.

Again, Estelle leaned toward the bear.

"Benny, let Estelle hold your bear a minute."

Benjamin looked at me.

I nodded to him.

Emily nodded, too.

Reluctantly, Benjamin put his bear into Estelle's outstretched arms.

She drew the bear tightly against her and sighed. At first Benjamin looked as if he might snatch it back.

But then he raced away, suddenly free for the first time in six months.

He played with both hands, like a wild man, while beside us on the bench Estelle grew quieter and quieter.

She lay in Officer Henky's arms but her entire world had become Benjamin's bear. As much as Benny loved that bear, he had never loved it the way Estelle loved it.

We talked softly with Officer Henky. He told us about being a policeman and about how he'd found Estelle and we told him about Mama and Papa and the bear business and about Emily's library and how we'd fixed it up in the shop window.

I didn't want the afternoon to end. I didn't want the moment to come when we had to ask for the bear back. But I knew the time would come. And I knew we would have to ask. And I hated myself for making Benny give up the bear in the first place. Because when the time did come, Benny, with his bear in tow, and Emily and I, we'd head straight back to our own private street of gold, straight back to our lucky life.

But what about Estelle? Where would she be going? To an orphanage. Alone. Empty-handed.

It just didn't seem right.

CHAPTER TWENTY~ONE

BENJAMIN HAD CLIMBED UP on the bench and wormed his way between Emily and Officer Henky. He needed to touch the bear for reassurance and Estelle happily shared with him. They played together quietly, the bear now the center of both of their worlds.

Officer Henky broke the spell.

"Estelle," he said. "We have to get you back home."

She turned her dark eyes to him. She said more with those eyes than I would ever know how to say with words.

"You need to give the bear back to Benjamin," Officer Henky said quietly.

Now Benjamin had his arms out.

Estelle stroked the bear. She held its face between her hands. She gave no indication that she was ever going to let it go.

But then she kissed Benny's bear on the tip of its nose, hugged it once more, and handed it over.

Officer Henky stood. Estelle clung to his neck.

"Thank you, Benjamin," Officer Henky said.

And they started away.

Benny climbed into Emily's lap, cradling his bear.

Officer Henky strode across the grass, heading down Sullivan Hill.

And then Benjamin was wriggling out of Emily's arms. He dropped off the bench, racing after Officer Henky.

And just like that, Benjamin handed the bear up to Estelle.

He came racing back, took my hand, and said, "I go home, Joe."

"Not just yet," I said. "There's a place I've been meaning to show you."

As I led the way to the waterfall, I kept thinking about Benjamin and suddenly how free he was, released from the burden of carrying his bear.

What bear had I been carrying, I wondered. And what would it take for me to let it go?

JANIE

They had guests from time to time under the bridge. Children who wandered there by accident, children who had a home, who belonged to families, families who wanted them. Janie was one such guest.

She lived on High Street and she loved two things: birds and horses. At two years she barely spoke and what few words she knew sounded strictly jabber to everyone but her mother.

Janie had gone to sleep in her mother's bed. She slept soundly while her brothers played in the parlor, while her baby sister fussed with colic, fussed so hotly that the eldest brother had been sent to fetch a remedy at the druggist and had, in his hurry, left the door to the apartment ajar. Janie, waking to see a brightly feathered bird fly past her window, rose, and in her nightclothes and bare feet followed the flitting bird.

Brr . . . brr . . . brr . . .
past the kitchen window.

The chubby feet padded through the kitchen and, finding the door open, raced outside in the fading light, calling,

Brr . . . ,
chasing after those bright feathers.

The parrot led her on her first solo outing into the

world, north and west and north and west. And finally to the bridge, where the parrot dove and perched on an ash can. Within moments Janie appeared, standing in her nightclothes, her pale hair fuzzy and wild with chasing parrots in the August night. She pointed to the parrot and called,

Brr . . . brr . . . brr . . . ,

smiling a cooey smile, her eyes wide with wonder. And deaf Frances, who had always wanted a sister, who had always been a little jealous of Helen and Nina, Frances read Janie's lips and understood, scooped her up, carried her close to the parrot.

She doesn't belong here, *Karl said.* We have to take her back.

But Frances looked away and would not read his lips because she did not wish to hear what he had to say. The children stared at one another because Janie was too little to know how to find home and Frances was too stubborn to release her now that she had her.

We have to take her to the police, *said Karl.*

The police!

Are you crazy, *Mattie said.* We can't show up at the police with a baby. First they'll arrest us for kidnapping and then they'll send us all to homes.

Frances, with her funny voice that sounded like it came through a megaphone with a rag stuffed inside it, said,

I'll look after her.

And Janie rested her head on Frances's shoulder and sighed and patted the cheek of her little adopted mother.

We keep her through the night, and leave her outside a police station tomorrow, *Karl said.*

And they all agreed. So Janie, delighted with her new family, delighted to be petted the way her baby sister was petted at home, played with the children under the bridge. Every now and then she'd tug on Frances's hand and pull her near the

Brr . . . brr . . .

and Frances, like a fairy godmother, obliged the child by bringing her close to the parrot, moving slowly, which kept the bird on its best behavior.

And as the children rose in the morning and stretched and scratched and searched the sky for a hint of what they might expect from the day, whether they should plan on getting wet or sweating in the brick city, Frances took little Janie in her arms and began making her way south and east and south and east, just far enough from the bridge that no policeman would connect this lost baby with those lost children.

But before Frances could find a policeman, Janie patted her cheek and, pointing to the firehouse, called,

Orsie . . . orsie . . . orsie . . . ,

and when Frances tried to carry her away, Janie made her body straight and slid out of the tired arms and ran toward the firehouse, toward the enormous doors.

Only moments before a call had come in, a house on fire.

As Janie ran toward them, the wide doors swung open and the horses in their brass jewels, their nostrils flaring, pawed at the firehouse floor. And Frances, understanding at once the baby's peril, cried out like a mute swan and raced to sweep up the child before the horses trampled her.

At the last moment the fire chief saw Frances, and then Janie.

"Hold!" *he ordered.* "Hold!"

As the chief raced toward Janie, Frances slid back into the shadows.

The fire chief lifted Janie into his arms, shaking his head.

What if? What if I hadn't seen her in time?

Janie vanished into the fire station only to appear minutes later, crowing with glee in the fire chief's arms.

He brought her home, as Frances trailed behind them, watching, watching, watching until the baby was safely back in her mother's embrace, her mother, her mother who wept with gratitude.

And Frances wept, too.

CHAPTER TWENTY~TWO

UNCLE MEYER PROPOSED MARRIAGE to Lizzie Kaplan and she accepted.

Uncle Meyer said, "There's no point waiting."

I thought about The Queen and her advice not to fall in love. It was too late for Uncle Meyer and Lizzie Kaplan. But I think The Queen would have approved anyway.

Aunt Lena traveled by rail from Chicago to Brooklyn, bringing Mary with her to attend the wedding.

Aunt Zelda arrived at the hall, her face painted brighter than The Queen's ever had been.

Everyone who had climbed the stairs from Tompkins Avenue to our flat over the last two months, the Rostowskys, Pauline and her Russian, even Mr. Kromer, that's who Aunt Lizzie wanted at her wedding. To her list of invitees she added the outside and inside seamstresses, even the cutters, but although they all gathered in front of the hall to wish her well, none of them came in for the ceremony. Instead, they presented the couple with a quilt for their bridal bed. Each had made a different square, each square was a variation on a Michtom bear.

The wedding ceremony wasn't a religious service but certain things Lizzie insisted on. Like the wineglass wrapped in white cloth.

"To remember," she said, "that even in times of joy, life holds sorrow."

Uncle Meyer stomped on the glass with that banana foot of his. The glass never stood a chance.

When Lizzie was asked if she'd take Uncle Meyer for her husband, she started crying so hard she couldn't say "I do." All the women started crying then, even Aunt Beast. And when Mama shouted, "She does, she does," Lizzie nodded like a horse in a stall and all the tears got swallowed up by laughter.

And then Uncle Meyer and Aunt Lizzie kissed and waved good-bye and climbed into a white carriage outside the hall and trotted away. Uncle Meyer had arranged that . . . the white horses, a white carriage, white flowers. They looked like a dream, prancing off in their chariot into the setting sun.

The moment the newlyweds left for their honeymoon, Papa and Mama announced that the celebration had only just begun. Uncle Meyer and Aunt Lizzie's wedding guests would be Rose and Morris Michtom's guests now, for the remainder of the evening. And where would we have our party?

On Coney Island!

We were going to Coney Island!

Papa turned to me. "You will join the rest of us, Joseph? I know you've recently taken in the sights at Coney but . . . oh, and we were planning on riding the trolley . . . but if you'd rather walk . . ."

"Very funny, Papa."

CHAPTER TWENTY~THREE

THE TROLLEY CARRIED US TO CONEY ISLAND and dropped us outside the entrance to Luna Park. This time I wasn't faint with hunger. This time I wasn't alone. I had wished for Emily back then. Now, not only did I have Emily with me, I had half of Brooklyn.

As the sun set, Papa paid our admissions.

We moved in a straggling mass through the gates of Luna Park, entering a world of fantasy. I looked back, just for a moment, at where I had stood the last time I'd come to Coney.

Emily grabbed my hand and pulled me through the gate.

Every archway, and there were hundreds of them, arches to our right, arches to our left, arches behind and in front of us, every arch glittered with lights. Every building glowed. Lights traced the outlines of pagodas and onion-shaped roofs.

I could smell hot dogs. I could smell the sea. I could smell wild animals and the sugar that was Turkish taffy. It was the end of August, soon a new month would begin, soon it would be autumn. But tonight it was still August, still completely, undeniably summer.

So many sounds, children shouting, laughter, the ticket sellers beckoning, a band playing, the *hummm* of motors.

I felt wrapped in Luna Park. Like a frankfurter in a bun.

"Papa," I said. "I'm hungry."

"The first order of business then," Papa called, "is to feed everyone!"

We stood on line. Papa went first and last, to square things with the vendor. He treated everyone, every last sticky bun, every last ear of roasted corn was paid for out of Papa's pocket. I looked into the faces of my parents, my parents who had worked so hard their entire lives, my parents who had gotten the lucky break that everyone in Brooklyn dreamed about. Their faces beamed. There was no worry, not a line of trouble to be seen. This evening promised to cost a fortune but Mama and Papa, they had made a fortune and it pleased them, I could see how much it pleased them, to share it.

We ate until our stomachs pressed against our waistbands.

And then came the real fun. The posters promised thirty-nine thrilling shows in Luna Park alone. Each sounded too good to miss but I knew, moving with this crowd we'd never see even a quarter of the sights. Riding the chutes, traveling to the moon, those were the things I most wanted to do. Emily, too. Benjamin said he wanted to "see da lelephants."

Lately, all Benjamin talked about were elephants. I hoped my parents didn't get any more bright ideas.

THE CITY of Venice dazzled. In the water, gondoliers stood in their boats and sang, waiting for passengers. The lake reflected thousands of lights. It looked like a piece of the sky had dropped onto Coney Island.

"Look, Morris," Mama said. "The lights, they're like stars."

"You want to go in the gondola, Rose?"

Papa wrapped his arms around Mama and Mama leaned against him. "Maybe not tonight. Maybe we'll come again, Morris. We'll come like these young couples do and you can court me."

I'd been holding my breath but Mama hadn't let me down. She knew what we wanted and she knew how to get it for us. We did not want to waste our Coney Island night on a guy in a striped shirt booming Italian love songs in our ears. Not even Pauline and her Russian wanted that. What we wanted was across the path from Venice. We wanted the "Trip to the Moon."

Jacob Rostowsky, flanked by his parents, kept asking about the moon and was it really made of cheese. Maybe some other time I would have been annoyed. But I wasn't about to let anything spoil Coney for me.

Aunt Lena spoke softly to Mary, who seemed a little frightened by the idea of space travel. My sister took Mary's hand and held it reassuringly.

We'd been standing on line about ten minutes when Aunt

Beast caught sight of a man in an open booth on the opposite side of the path. He was drawing a portrait in charcoal. She studied him while he worked. She pushed her way forward for a better view of him.

Her face went white.

A cloud of worry crossed Mama's face. "What's the matter, Zelda, dear? Are you feeling ill?"

Aunt Beast pointed to the artist in the booth, her finger shaking. "It's my . . . it's . . . it's Izzy. That's Izzy. . . ."

Papa stared. "No, Zelda, it can't be. How could it be?"

"It is," Aunt Beast said. "You think I don't know him? He's older. But it's Izzy! It is! That's him. That's Izzy!"

"Izzy's gone," Mama said.

"But he's there," Aunt Beast cried, trembling. "It's Izzy. And if Izzy's alive . . . maybe . . ."

"Shah, Zelda," Papa said. "The boy's dead. They're both dead. All you're doing is getting yourself worked up, making a scene. That can't really be Izzy. It's just someone who looks like him. That's all."

Aunt Beast, up-and-coming real-estate tycoon, looking at all the strangers in line staring at her, looking at the artist in the booth, who, from a different angle, didn't quite look like Uncle Izzy after all, Aunt Beast realized Papa was right. Her son was gone. Her husband was gone. This man couldn't really be Izzy. And she *was* making a scene.

I could see Aunt Beast struggling to regain her composure as the Michtom family, along with their guests and a dozen or so others, swept to the front of the line and boarded a space-ship to the moon.

No sooner had we settled onto the ride when the ship began to vibrate and suddenly great wings rose from either side. The wings lifted and fell, lifted and fell, like a powerful bird, bearing us up. Below us sprawled all of Coney Island. Then as the ship's wings flapped we passed over the lighted buildings of Manhattan, and finally our spaceship vanished inside the clouds.

In a matter of minutes we landed on the moon. Moon people poured forward to greet us. Tiny moon people who escorted us out of our ship and led us inside the moon where the floor rocked and the walls dripped.

Papa carried Benjamin.

Jacob kept saying, "Is this the real moon? Is this the real moon?" His parents tried to calm him without ruining the ride for the rest of us.

Little Mary's eyes never blinked the entire time.

When we exited the ride, having walked through the entire moon, we passed under an arched door and found ourselves back in the night glow of Luna Park.

"Again!" Benjamin shouted.

"I'm going to get a closer look. I need to be sure," Aunt Beast said.

Papa said, "Look at you, Zelda. You've never been better. Don't open old wounds. The two of them are gone. A half-dozen witnesses saw them go under. It won't do you any good talking with this man. He can't bring your son back."

But Aunt Beast wouldn't be stopped.

And as we approached the booth, Mama gasped.

"Oh my God. Morris," she whispered. "It *is* Izzy."

And it wasn't until that moment that I realized he was the man from the beach. The man with the gray goatee and the beret. No wonder I hadn't been afraid of him. He'd offered to take me home that night. Said he had a son once. The boy he was talking about. It was my cousin. Stephen.

IT WAS EASY to tell when Uncle Izzy recognized Aunt Beast.

He froze in his tracks, midpatter.

He had his pencil poised.

His hands started shaking.

"Zelda?" he whispered.

"It really is you," Aunt Beast said. "But how? How can you be alive?"

"Zelda," Uncle Izzy repeated.

"Who do you think? You were expecting the tzar, maybe?" Aunt Beast asked.

Uncle Izzy stared at her for what seemed like forever, though it couldn't really have been more than a minute. He looked at the crowd around her. The Rostowskys, Pauline and her Russian, Aunt Lena and little Mary.

Everyone felt his panic. But no one moved away. Like coming suddenly on a trolley accident. Expecting everything to be normal, expecting an evening of fun, and suddenly thrust inside a tragedy.

All the color had drained from Uncle Izzy's face. He looked like a dead man. "What are you doing here?" he whispered.

"What did you do with Stephen?" Aunt Beast demanded. "Where's Stephen?"

"Don't. Don't, Zelda." Uncle Izzy moaned. "He's gone. He's gone."

Aunt Beast glared at him. Defiant.

"Tell me what you did with my boy. He's alive, too, isn't he? Tell me where I can find Stephen!"

I looked at Emily. Now she knew who Stephen was.

"You disappeared," Aunt Beast said. "Ten years!"

"You were better off that way." Uncle Izzy spoke in a whisper.

"How would you know?" Aunt Beast said, spitting each word out. "How could you possibly know? Ten years. And not a word."

"Look at you, Zelda. Tell me you're not better off," Uncle Izzy said.

"A lot you care," Aunt Beast said. "Where's my son?"

"Please, Zelda. Tell me. How have you been?"

A customer approached Uncle Izzy's booth, saw the crowd, and moved away.

"I've been working myself to an early grave," Aunt Beast answered. "All these years with no one to support me. All these years without my precious boy. He would be a man now. Eighteen years old. A man. Something his father never was."

Uncle Izzy touched his pencils gently. "I put every dime away. I meant to give it all to you. When I'd saved enough. I'll give you the money now, Zelda. It's not much but I always meant you should have it."

"Forget it. I don't need your lousy dimes."

Uncle Izzy looked down. Ashamed. After a moment he tried again. "How are your sisters?"

"Lena's there." Aunt Beast pointed to Aunt Mouse, who had moved away a distance to protect Mary. "Golda died," Aunt Beast said, like that was Uncle Izzy's fault, too.

"Golda? I never knew a woman strong as Golda. I'm sorry. When did it happen?"

"Last month."

"Last month? Oh, Zelda."

"Spare me your sympathy."

Aunt Beast glared.

"But you're doing okay, Zelda."

"No thanks to you."

"No, no thanks to me."

"But if Stephen's alive . . ."

"He's not alive, Zelda," Uncle Izzy said, shrinking into himself.

Uncle Izzy had talent. Hanging in his booth were portraits of women, men, children. A drawing of the Statue of Liberty. Several of the Brooklyn Bridge.

Aunt Beast studied a sketch of a boy with fair hair, capless, standing at the top of a staircase in his nightshirt.

"Stephen," she said. "All these years I never had a picture of him. You wouldn't let me get his photograph taken. You would paint him, you said. You never did."

"I couldn't paint him. I tried, I couldn't. There's only this."

He took down the sketch of my cousin in his nightshirt and gave it to Aunt Beast. His hands lingered on hers. She pulled away.

"How dare you, Izzy," she said. "How can I believe you? I don't think he's dead. You've kept him to yourself. All these years."

Aunt Beast's eyes flashed like pieces of steel.

Looking at Uncle Izzy's stricken face, I don't know how Aunt Beast could possibly believe that Stephen was still alive.

"Where is he?" Aunt Beast asked once more. "What did you do with him?"

At first it looked as if Uncle Izzy had lost his voice. He'd start to speak. Then stop. Start. Stop. Finally, looking away from us, he tried again.

"He's under the bridge," Uncle Izzy whispered.

"Under the bridge?"

"Brooklyn Bridge," Uncle Izzy said. "I buried him under the bridge . . . for all eternity he should haunt those murdering street kids who live there."

Uncle Izzy caught sight of Aunt Beast's face.

"Under the bridge," she said, horrified. "That's where you put your son to rest?"

Head down, he nodded. "I'm so sorry, Zelda."

CHAPTER TWENTY~FOUR

"I HOPE HE DOESN'T THINK he can get his hands on my money," Aunt Beast said.

"He didn't look well," observed Mr. Kromer as we moved under the dazzling lights toward the Shoot-the-Chutes.

"It's true," Papa said. "Close up I could see, too. He's not a well man."

"It's nice he gave you the portrait," Mama said.

"How can you," Aunt Beast hissed at Mama, indignant. "This is my son. This is all I have left of my son."

"It was his tragedy, too," Aunt Lena said.

Aunt Beast glared at her.

Despite Mama's protests, we took Benjamin on the Shoot-the-Chutes. He sat in Papa's lap and held on with both hands as we plunged down the slide in our boat, slammed into the water, then rose and fell, rose and fell, until the boat settled and the boatman steered us back to the platform.

"Again!" Benjamin yelled as we climbed out.

Mama, Aunt Beast, Aunt Mouse and Mary sat on a bench, gazing up at the Electric Tower. Thousands of lights in the tower, thousands of lights on lines leading from the tower, thousands and thousands of lights reflected in the fountains, turning night into day. Pauline and her Russian stood huddled together, apart from the rest of our group. Pauline clung to her husband, laughing softly. His head tilted, listening, holding her close against him.

Serenaded by Scinta's Band at the far end of the lake, we joined the line waiting to enter the Hippodrome.

Once we were seated inside, we watched the wild animal acts. Earlier this month one of the acrobats had fallen during a show, dying a few days later from his injuries. I watched with dread that we should witness anything else. Aunt Beast's scene with Uncle Izzy had been enough.

I wanted to forget all that. I wanted to be happy. I wanted Coney to be perfect. I wanted the lights to be so bright I'd be blind to everything outside the fantasy of Coney Island. Seeing Uncle Izzy hadn't quite ruined the night for me. Maybe for Aunt Beast the night was ruined, but not for me, not for the rest of us. Not quite.

PAULINE AND HER Russian left at around eleven-thirty, thanking Mama and Papa over and over for a wonderful time. Then they thanked me. Then Emily. They even thanked Benjamin.

I felt something shift inside me, watching them leave the park together. Pauline was all right. She'd always been all right. My problem with Pauline, it had been my problem. I knew that now.

It was nearly midnight. Benjamin's eyes drooped. Jacob sagged against Mr. Rostowsky. Mr. Kromer carried Mary.

"Time to go home?" Papa asked.

No one argued.

CHAPTER TWENTY~FIVE

AS WE HEADED DOWN the bright avenue of lights toward the exit, we passed Uncle Izzy's booth one last time. Even though the crowd had thinned, Luna Park still carried on. My uncle's booth, however, looked deserted. All of his artwork remained on the walls. His pencils still sat out. But there was no sign of Uncle Izzy.

"Where did he go?" Aunt Beast asked Papa.

A fortune-teller stood several booths over.

"You looking for Izzy?" she called.

Aunt Beast nodded.

"He's gone," the fortune-teller said.

Aunt Beast let out a scornful laugh. "I've heard that before."

The fortune-teller leaned out of her booth, eager to gossip. "No, I mean it. He's gone. For good. He said it was his lucky day. And then he just walked out of the park."

"What are you talking about?" Aunt Beast asked.

"He had a good day, maybe ten portraits. Most people aren't here to have a portrait made. They walk right past him. But today was good for him. And tonight, tonight he said he got really lucky."

Aunt Beast swayed, looking faint.

"You okay?" the fortune-teller asked. "You family or something?"

Aunt Beast nodded.

"Here, come on over. Sit down. Don't worry. I won't charge. Sit."

Aunt Beast looked up into the fortune-teller's eyes. "Tell me what happened."

"He . . . say, you must be related to his dead wife. I see the resemblance."

"His . . . ?"

"She was a good-looking woman. Yeah. I can see. You look a lot like the pictures of her. He drew her over and over. She's been gone ten years. He never got over her. I figured that's what made him a little bit funny. You know? And his kid. The poor boy. He used to have a picture of the kid in his booth. It's gone now. I see the empty place where it used to hang."

Aunt Beast clutched the rolled-up sketch of Stephen.

"Cute little thing. I can't imagine how it tore him up, losing them both. Yeah, he needed some luck."

Papa brought a lemonade over from the concession and put it in Aunt Beast's hands. Now her hands were trembling. The way Uncle Izzy's had.

"Anyway," the fortune-teller said, "he had a crowd tonight. But after it quieted down he got strange. You know how he gets. Only tonight was much worse."

"How do you mean, strange?"

"I didn't pay that much attention. I had a line of customers, myself. People are dying to know when they're gonna make it big. They all want to be rich and famous."

"But you said he's gone. For good. How do you know?"

"He never leaves his booth without cleaning up. Never. Believe me. A real nice guy, Izzy. Most of the time. But, like I said, he got strange tonight. Started pacing inside his booth. He had a customer standing right there. Didn't even notice.

" 'Now I can die happy. Now I can die happy,' that's what he kept saying over and over. Then he just walked out. Down the avenue. The crowds parted for him. The lights shining so bright on him, just on him, like he was the star of the show or something. Like he was the only person in Luna Park."

"Emily," I whispered. "I think I know where Uncle Izzy went. I need to find him. Before he does something stupid. Tell Mama and Papa not to worry. I'll be back."

I could tell Emily wanted to come.

But I wouldn't upset Mama and Papa again by disappearing without an explanation. Emily had to stay. To tell them I was all right.

LEAVING THE LIGHTS of Luna Park behind, I ran, afraid I would be too late.

But I wasn't. Uncle Izzy, he was exactly where I thought I'd find him. Exactly where he'd found me. Away from the lights. Sitting alone on the beach.

"Uncle Izzy?"

"Who's there?"

"It's me, Joseph. Joseph Michtom."

"Ah, Joseph. You're all grown up."

I sat down beside him. It was different from the last time I'd been to Coney. I was different.

"I'm glad you're okay," I said.

"I'm glad *you're* okay," Uncle Izzy said. "I always wondered what happened to you. It was wrong for me to leave you. Such a little boy. But the police were there. All gathered around you. I knew they'd get you home. I knew they wouldn't let those street boys hurt you the way they hurt Stephen."

"Uncle Izzy, the street boys didn't hurt Stephen."

"You wouldn't know," Uncle Izzy said. "You were just a little thing. You can't imagine how evil those boys are. Pushing your cousin into the river."

"The street boys didn't push Stephen," I said. "No one pushed Stephen. He jumped."

"What do you mean?" Uncle Izzy turned to me. His eyes focused on my face.

"It was some boys Stephen knew who started it. When they saw Stephen they came over. They pushed him around. Teased him because his clothes were so fancy. They said he made them look bad."

Uncle Izzy continued to stare at me.

"I tried pulling them away," I said. "One boy shoved me and I fell on the ground. Another one, he snatched Stephen's hat. Stephen was afraid Aunt Zelda would be angry if he lost that hat. So when the boy threw Stephen's hat into the river, Stephen had to go after it. He told me. He told me to stay right where I was. Not to move. Not an inch. I always listened to Stephen but I shouldn't have listened to him. I watched him jump into the water. I did what he said, Uncle Izzy. Instead of running to tell you right away, I stayed just where Stephen told me and I didn't move. The kids who had pushed Stephen around, they ran away as soon as he jumped. A couple of street kids, when they realized Stephen was in trouble, they came to get you."

"They came to taunt me."

"No, Uncle Izzy, they came to get you. They wanted you to save Stephen."

"This can't be true."

Uncle Izzy turned away. I watched his profile in the dark.

"It is true," I said. "I swear it."

"All these years I've been . . ."

"What?"

"All these years," Uncle Izzy said. "I blamed them for Stephen's death. The street kids. I took it out on them."

"They were only trying to help, Uncle Izzy."

My uncle let out a ragged breath. "By the time I got into the water Stephen had gone under. I couldn't find him at first.

I tried. And then, when I did find him, it was too late. I carried his body out of the water while the police, while everyone fussed over you. You were screaming. Such a quiet boy. But you weren't quiet then. As I carried Stephen away, that's all I heard. I heard you screaming.

"It's funny. I had you that day because your mother had gone into labor and Zelda told me to look after you. It was my day off. I wanted to paint. But I had to do what Zelda told me. Stephen was so grown up. He loved looking after you. I wasn't watching."

Uncle Izzy took off his beret and twisted it in his hands.

"I nearly drowned trying to find him. Poor Stephen. In all those clothes his mother made him wear he didn't stand a chance."

Uncle Izzy was quiet for a moment. I heard only the sound of the sea, the restless sound of the sea.

"Carrying Stephen's body, I inched away, away from the police. I handled some real estate down there near the bridge. I knew where to hide with him. I only left him long enough to go home and get his nightshirt. I slipped into our flat while Zelda was with your mother, helping with the birth."

Emily, I thought. Stephen died the day Emily was born. I didn't remember that.

"I needed to get out of the flat before Zelda caught me. I raced back to Stephen, stripped off his wet clothes, dried him, dressed him in his nightgown. Later, while Brooklyn slept, while Zelda got the news from the police, while your mother held her new baby, I dug. There was already some excavation going on under the bridge. I chased away the couple street kids under there, and I dug, deeper than the excavation the city was doing. Deeper and deeper. Deep enough for Stephen. My poor son. I buried Stephen under the bridge.

"I kept out of sight for years. Moved down here to Coney. It was different down here then. Nobody bothered you. And all this time I never saw your aunt."

"She never crossed the bridge until this summer," I said. "She hated the river. Because of Stephen. Because of you. We all hated the river."

"I'd hoped she'd think we'd both drowned. That I'd drowned trying to save him."

"She did. We all did."

I didn't know if he remembered sitting with me on this beach before. We'd both been a little out of our minds that night. Now he was a little more out of his. And I, I was a little less out of mine.

Sitting on the beach at Coney Island with my uncle, I knew, finally, just like that, I was finished carrying my bear.

Grabbing fistfuls of sand, I let the grains slip in two thin columns back onto the beach.

"What will you do now?" I asked.

Uncle Izzy looked out at the black Atlantic and shrugged.

"Give it all to Zelda, I guess," he said. "Give her everything. Make it easier for me to move on, start over."

I brushed the remaining sand off my hands, put an arm across Uncle Izzy's shoulders, and leaned into him. It felt good the way he leaned right back.

INTRUSION

Police arrived and suddenly it became impossible to live under the bridge. Men dug with shovels, their clothes stained with sweat. They left a sour smell under the bridge that had nothing to do with children. Every morning the diggers returned, early, so early, with the gray light of dawn.

So the children had to wake in the middle of the night and kick their bedding out of sight into the deepest recesses under the bridge and melt away until darkness returned and the diggers left.

They were excavating a pit, a great oozing gouge in the earth. The children had to crowd together at night and sleep as far as possible from the rim of the hole because the sound that came from it filled them with horror, the sound of the earth screaming.

Each day the men dug deeper, wider. Each day they broadened the gash. And each night the tormented earth cried louder and louder until even the boy with the violin could not comfort the children. They didn't know how they could continue to live with the earth in so much pain right there, under their worn bodies.

The Radiant Boy came every night now, every night, but he paid no attention to the children.

The Radiant Boy rose out of the gash in the earth and hovered there, hovered, hovered there over the hole, his mouth wide open, and the sound of the screaming earth, it came from him.

GOING DEEP

And even Mattie, who had been driven by madness, his father's and his own, to find shelter under the bridge, and Otto, who had slept beside the corpse of the hermit, Mattie and Otto put their hands over their ears and rocked back and forth in pain.

The police dug and dug and dug into the heart of the earth. And each night the Radiant Boy hovered over it, howling his banshee howl.

THE DISCOVERY

On the third day the police found the skeleton of a boy buried deep, deep beneath the bridge, and they handed his bones up. Every bone, carefully. They handed up those bones and the worm-eaten nightgown. And still a bit of fine blond hair. And the police, when the gruesome task ended, filled in the hole, carried away their shovels, and didn't come back.

THE RETURN

And that night, at last, the earth was at peace.

The stars pierced the velvet night like dressmaker pins. And as the children returned to the bridge, above them, a stairway appeared, stretching down through the sky. Down, down, down, until it touched the earth, touched exactly there, right at the bridge.

A stairway so broad that all the poor of New York could have climbed it, shoulder to shoulder.

Up that shining path climbed a small, golden-haired boy in a white nightshirt. In silence the children watched. The boy with the violin had been so eager for evening, to feel the bow in his hand, so eager to hear his instrument sing. But watching this small, barefooted child ascend the stairway, the boy let the violin rest at his side.

What was human music compared with this? Even music played on an instrument made by the son of Stradivarius. No human sound would be right, now.

And so the children stood in silence, until the white of the nightgown became lost in the milky cluster of stars.

And the stairway faded.

And these are the joys which Luna Park offers to every stranger within its gates for the dime which it costs to get in.

—THE BROOKLYN DAILY EAGLE

CHAPTER TWENTY~SIX

THE GUYS, THEY SAY I'M LUCKY. And I know I am. I know it. But sometimes you have to make your own luck. Like my parents making the Teddy Bear. Like Uncle Meyer and Aunt Lizzie making a life together. Like Aunt Lena and Mary. And Aunt Beast.

Whatever kind of luck, the luck you make, or the luck that makes you, the way I see it, luck will only get you so far. You got to go the rest of the way on your own two feet.

All of Uncle Izzy's worldly goods arrived at Aunt Beast's flat on the Lower East Side a few days later. Before that day ended Aunt Beast had given away most of those worldly goods. In crowded East Side flats, where people slept on boards balanced between two chairs, where the smell of cabbage seeped out of open windows, where always, somewhere, someone's baby was squealing, fine portraits made by Uncle Izzy hung on peeling paper, on sagging walls. Aunt Beast gave away every painting Uncle Izzy had done of her as a young woman. And nearly everything else.

She kept only the sketch of Stephen in his nightshirt. Only that.

Papa asked for and received the painting of three sisters and their little brother playing in an apple orchard in Russia.

And I, I took a painting of the Statue of Liberty, the one that showed a small boat rowing past, the oarsman looking over his shoulder toward shore, no longer needing a beam of light to guide him. It was sunrise and his bare eyes were enough to bring him safely home.

AUTHOR'S NOTE

The seed for this novel rests on page 36 of Bill Slavin's book, *Transformed, How Everyday Things Are Made.* Bill and I met at a conference in Atlanta in 2006. Before returning home, I purchased a copy of his book, which he kindly autographed.

Back in Vermont I read along happily about how baseballs were made, and chewing gum, and ships in a bottle, until I reached the section on stuffed bears. At the top of the page a brief historical note mentioned the first American teddy bear and its creator, Morris Michtom. Why that note awoke something in me is part of the mystery of the creative process. But I immediately put Bill's book down and started digging into the lives of the Michtom family.

Over time this is what I discovered. In 1888, at the age of eighteen, Morris Michtom married Rose Katz. The day after the wedding the newlyweds parted. While Rose waited in Russia, in the city of Minsk, Morris joined the migrating masses seeking a new life in America. Less than a year later Morris had saved enough to bring Rose over.

As the Michtom family grew, so did the immigrant population of New York City. Nearly every greenhorn experienced challenges: obstacles of language, poor health, clashing cultures, substandard housing, unemployment. Most managed to overcome those challenges. But some did not. Occasionally families unraveled. The city erected institutions to assist the struggling and the homeless, but sometimes people slipped through the cracks, either accidentally or with intention.

Like many immigrant couples, Rose and Morris Michtom could barely support their family on the slim profits of their candy and novelty shop. And then, one day, an editorial cartoon by Clifford Berryman appeared in the newspaper. It depicted President Theodore Roosevelt refusing to shoot a bear cub in a Mississippi swamp. The bear had been captured after enduring a long and bloody chase. Hunting guides summoned Roosevelt to make the kill. Theodore Roosevelt loved hunting, but he couldn't bring himself to shoot a wounded and tethered animal.

Rose and Morris Michtom easily identified with the defenseless cub in Berryman's cartoon. They remembered their early years in Russia, where the constant threat of persecution kept a majority of Jews fearing for their lives. Clifford Berryman's illustration of that frightened bear cub marked a change in fortune for the Michtom family.

Up until that time toy bears had been primarily made of wood or metal. The Michtoms' cloth bear with its movable arms, legs, and head was a novelty immediately embraced by the public. Before long women as well as children brought teddy bears, dressed exquisitely, to take tea at the finest restaurants, demanding the stuffed toys be treated as honored guests.

The dawn of the twentieth century saw a tide of optimism

wash over the United States. Families flocked to ball games, theaters, and the dazzling entertainments of new amusement centers like Luna Park and Dreamland. At such venues the poor rubbed elbows with the middle class and the wealthy. People from all walks of life strolled together on the same promenades, laughed brightly at the same wonders, cried with delight over the same pasteboard diversions.

This novel is a pasteboard diversion of a different sort. Though I used the Michtoms' success story as my inspiration, this book is entirely a work of fiction. *Brooklyn Bridge* is one writer's musing on what it might have been like in the early twentieth century to sometimes have too little, sometimes too much, and sometimes, to have it just right.

ACKNOWLEDGMENTS

Is it possible that any work of historical fiction can be written in isolation? This book took shape with the help of communities and individuals past and present. Over the last two years, so many people have given generously of their time and thought. I thank each of you for your patience, wisdom, vision, and kindness.

These are but a few of the many who contributed to the building of this particular stretch of the Brooklyn Bridge:

Justin Ferate, Leda Schubert, Liza Ketchum, Julie Reimer, Michael Waite, Simi Berman, Wendy Watson, Tink MacLean, Paul Zelinsky, Deborah Hallin, Precious Walker-Jones, the staff of the Brooklyn Public Library, the staff of the Brooklyn Museum of Art, the staff of the Brooklyn Historical Society, Alvin and Geraldine Abarbanel Donald, Liz Szabla, Leslie Budnick, Rachel and Randy Hesse, and the entire Michtom family, particularly Paula Michtom, Joan Michtom, Jessica Lauria, and Elinor Gabriel.

A separate acknowledgment must go to Jean Feiwel, the genius erector of so many bridges, with heartfelt thanks for welding this steel and soldering these bolts.

WELCOME TO
Coney Island

RIDES AND ATTRACTIONS

This smiling face is the "funny face" logo of Steeplechase Park,
a beloved Coney Island amusement park from 1897 to 1964.

Surf Avenue, Coney Island, N.Y.

OUTLINE MAP

OF THE

BOROUGH OF BROOKLYN

CITY OF NEW YORK

Upper

Gowanus Bay

The Narrows

BAY RIDGE

Third Ave.

Fourth Ave.

Greenu
Cemet

NEW UTRECHT

Gravesend
Bay

GRAVESEND

Ocean Parkway

FLAT

CONEY ISLAND

Surf Ave.

(8)

Atlantic Ocean